PRAISE FOR UNPAC

Curl up by your holiday fire with this charming tale. *Unpacking Christmas* will delight you.

— RACHEL HAUCK, *NEW YORK TIMES* BESTSELLING AUTHOR

Beth Vogt is an author I look to not only for a delightful story, but one that moves me and stays in my heart.

— SUSAN MAY WARREN, MULTI-AWARD-WINNING & BESTSELLING AUTHOR

Whether you're already a fan of the Thatcher Sister series or this is your first introduction, you're in for a treat! Author Beth Vogt tackles real-life issues as a family chooses love over hurt and uncovers the true spirit of Christmas in a story that is un-put-downable. This is everything a Christmas novella should be.

— EDIE MELSON, AWARD-WINNING AUTHOR & DIRECTOR OF THE BLUE RIDGE MOUNTAINS CHRISTIAN WRITERS CONFERENCE

Unpacking Christmas is the one present you need this season! Reuniting with the Thatcher sisters is like visiting old friends, complete with crackling fires and hot chocolate, love, and laughter. Beth Vogt has gifted us a sweet story filled with poignant moments, and the reminder that nothing is more important than family. Savor this one and add it to your Christmas wish list.

— CATHERINE WEST, AWARD-WINNING AUTHOR

UNPACKING CHRISTMAS

A THATCHER SISTERS CHRISTMAS NOVELLA

BETH K. VOGT

NEVER DOOR PRESS

To Fran
Years ago, when we first met, I hoped we'd become friends.
There's no way to count all the memories we've made
through the years – all the ways you've blessed my life.
Your friendship is one of God's best gifts to me.

1

*T*hanksgiving Day. Tradition demanded the day's focus was on being grateful. And as both the wife and mom in the Thatcher family, I was. But throughout the day, in between remembering all the reasons I was thankful, the words, *"Tell them,"* replayed in my mind. Don and I needed to tell them while the family was all here together.

But announcing our news to Johanna and Jillian and Payton was more difficult than I'd expected. And so, it was back to being thankful. Again.

If someone asked me what one thing I was most thankful for today, I'd tell them it was the drama-free scene right here in my kitchen.

My daughters had been together from mid-morning to late afternoon, and there'd been no snark. No irritated looks tossed back and forth between the trio. No chilly silence. Johanna hadn't hassled Payton about how many sugars she'd dumped into her cups of coffee. Jillian hadn't needed to referee any verbal skirmishes between her sisters.

With our Thanksgiving meal finished, the kitchen was crowded, couples working to clear away the mess. Johanna and Beckett washed serving utensils and pots. Jillian and Geoff loaded the dishwasher. Payton and Zach put away leftovers.

The family scene was threaded through with laughter, punctuating the lack of tension as everyone worked together, instead of squaring off with one another because someone was annoyed, offended, or outright angry.

So many good memories were tucked inside this house. Some heartbreaking ones too.

And some of the best memories had been made in the last two years.

Johanna leaned close to Beckett as he whispered something in her ear, her platinum blonde hair pulled back in a low ponytail. She grinned, splashing a bit of soapy water in his face. He caught her closer with a playful growl, droplets of water clinging to his dark hair.

Those two. So obviously in love with one another —and still leaving us all guessing as to whether they'd ever get married or not after reconciling with one another after Ellison's birth.

Johanna gave Beckett a quick kiss and stepped away from the sink, drying her hands on a dish towel. "I'd better check on Dad and Ellison."

"I'm sure they're fine downstairs." I gave the island one last swipe with a damp rag and centered the vase of flowers Jillian and Geoff had presented me that morning—all golds and yellows and oranges. "Your dad loves spending time with his only granddaughter— even more than he loves spending time with Winston."

"Just don't tell Winston—he'll put on his best doggie pout." Jillian shook her head, offering me a grin.

"I'm surprised how good your dog is with a rambunctious two-year-old." Johanna folded the dish towel, laying it on the counter next to the drying pots and pans.

"Winnie would never hurt Ellison." Jillian shut the dishwasher and turned it on, running her fingers through her short blonde hair—her chosen style now, no longer caused by cancer. The low hum became the mechanical background music in the kitchen. "And you and Beckett were both so patient, teaching Ellison to be gentle with him."

"Except for that one episode." Johanna grimaced. "Poor guy. All he did was whimper until we realized she had both fists wrapped around his eyebrows."

Jillian's eyes lit up as Johanna shared the memory. Laughter and happiness surrounded her most days. Such a change from two years ago.

Johanna and Jillian had rediscovered their close relationship after Johanna's unexpected pregnancy— discovered after she and Beckett had broken up—and

Jillian's infertility created an emotional impasse between them.

Had Jillian's faith caused the change? Or the fact that Jillian and Geoff had tabled the decision about having children during the past two years? Whatever the reason, it was good to see my middle daughter happy. Content.

With a swish of the door and a giggle from our granddaughter, Don entered the kitchen, carrying Ellison piggyback.

"Heather, this little girl wants something to drink." He deposited her in one of the chairs in the breakfast nook. "And Winston is enjoying time in the backyard."

"I'll get her something, Mom." Beckett removed a lime-green sippy cup from the cupboard. "Water, juice, or milk, Jo?"

"Whichever one she wants."

"Ellison?"

"Juice, Daddy."

"What do we say, sweetheart?"

"Please." Ellison tilted her head and smiled, prompting Beckett to drop a kiss on top of her strawberry blonde hair.

"Anyone else want something to drink?"

"Just worry about Ellison, Beck. We can get what we need." Johanna sat beside her daughter, tucking a curl behind her ear. "But thanks for asking."

"Anyone want to play a board game?" Zach closed the fridge door, the leftovers all stored away.

"When's the next football game?" Don glanced at the floral clock in the breakfast nook.

"We can always have the game on in the background while we play Codenames or Catan."

"Sounds good. And then we can have some leftovers before anyone heads home."

Payton groaned. "Dad, we just got everything put away."

"But the leftovers are the best part of Thanksgiving."

To the casual observer, we looked like the stereotypical happy family. But then, most people didn't know about the secrets that had threatened our relationships. The choices that had almost torn our family apart. The losses. The heartaches each one of my daughters still carried.

Don hugged Payton, saying something only she could hear and making her laugh. My daughters didn't realize how lucky they were to have such a good dad. Or maybe they did. I was thankful their memories of their dad were so different than mine.

And now we were all here . . . well, all of us except Pepper. I could only be grateful for the memories we'd given her before she died at sixteen. The love she'd experienced as one of the Thatcher sisters in her all-too-short life.

Tell them.

Don and I had discussed it all again last night— that if the opportunity presented itself today, we'd take advantage of it.

I met Don's gaze. Raised my eyebrows.

He mimicked my expression.

Was that a yes? A no?

I widened my eyes . . . and Don mirrored my expression again.

"Mom. Dad. What is going on? You look like two mimes doing a poorly rehearsed mirror routine."

Johanna's question caused Payton to giggle.

I guess we weren't so subtle after all.

"Dad and I want to talk to you all about something."

"Is that what all the eyebrow raising and eye widening was about?"

"I was trying to figure out if now was the right time . . ." My voice trailed off as all three girls fixed their gazes on me.

"Is everything okay?" Jillian leaned into Geoff, who wrapped an arm around her waist. "You're . . . not sick, are you?"

With all the upheaval in our family in recent years, including her breast cancer diagnosis, it wasn't surprising Jillian would expect the worst.

Everyone stepped closer to one another. Stilled. An emotional circling of the wagons.

What we were about to tell them was a *change*, not a crisis. I needed the girls to see this change was good.

"Your dad and I are selling the house."

My announcement was met by silence. Unblinking stares from Johanna. Jillian. Payton.

"Can I have more juice, please?" Ellison's sweet voice broke through the tension.

"Just a minute, sweetheart."

"Sure, Elle."

Beckett's and Johanna's conflicting responses collided.

"I'll get her something." Beckett stepped away from Johanna, but not before he gave her hand a quick squeeze. "Just half a glass."

Johanna refocused on me. "Why . . . why are you thinking about selling the house?"

"We're not thinking about it anymore. We did that for the last six months. More like a year." I paused, but Don seemed happy to let me handle explaining our decision. "I guess the main reason is we don't need this big house."

"But you just put the deck in a couple of years ago." This from Payton.

"And the deck adds to the resale value of the house."

"Isn't selling the house going to be a lot of work?"

"It's still a seller's market. Our Realtor says—"

"You already have a Realtor?" Jillian's voice was higher-pitched than normal.

"Yes. You need one to sell a house." I tried to soften my words with a laugh. "She's the wife of one of your dad's former colleagues. She's very good and we like working with her."

"How quickly do you plan to put the house on the

market?" Johanna, ever the calm one, was fact-gathering.

"The second week of December."

"That soon?"

"Well, there's no need to wait, especially since we've already bought a house."

"What?" Jillian's question came out on a gasp.

"You've bought another house?" Payton gripped Zach's hand.

"We know it's a little backwards, but we've been casually looking and found a perfect house with less square footage than what we have here. A wonderful view of Pikes Peak. Things are moving so quickly right now, we decided to put an offer on it and—surprise!— it was accepted. We close in early February."

"You're serious . . ." Payton's blue-green gaze— always a reminder of Pepper—darted between me and her dad, as if expecting one of us to change the story.

"Very much so." Don's voice was firm.

"Fortunately, we painted both the interior and exterior of the house last summer and we selected neutral colors for the rooms just in case we decided to sell. The Realtor told me what to do since we're showing the house during the holidays. Normally, we don't go crazy with Christmas decorations. Your dad and I are trying to decide if we're going to put up a tree or not."

"No Christmas tree?" Jillian's tone was similar to Ellison's when her parents told her no.

"Again, the Realtor recommended it. Or she said

we should put up a smaller one with white lights. No ornaments."

"Your Realtor sounds like a Scrooge." Johanna crossed her arms. "Bah, humbug."

"Jo, our decision to sell the house doesn't stop you from celebrating the holidays. You can still decorate your house however you want to."

"But we always open gifts here. And have Christmas dinner."

"And we still will. Christmas is on a Saturday this year, so we won't show the house from the Wednesday before through the weekend. And who knows? Maybe we'll sell the house fast."

We seemed to have switched roles—having to explain ourselves to Johanna, Jillian, and Payton—as if Don and I were the children and they were the parents.

Don stepped next to me, resting his hand on my shoulder. He hadn't said much up until now, but his touch was a gentle reminder we'd agreed on this decision.

We'd bought a new house. Signed a contract with our Realtor, Tracey, to sell this one.

Did the girls even remember we'd decided to sell this house once before and then backed out when Pepper died when she and Payton were juniors in high school?

This time, we weren't going to change our minds.

THEY'D BEEN HOME FOR SEVERAL HOURS, AND PAYTON still grappled with her parents' decision to sell their house. She'd ignored Johanna's texts and Jillian's phone call, needing to make sense of it herself before she could talk to her sisters.

Life was changing so much—more than Johanna and Jillian and Mom and Dad realized.

"Do you think we should have told them?" Payton sat on the edge of their bed and pulled a pillow into her lap, wrapping her arms around it. Laz, their big black mutt, settled at her feet.

"Payton, if you're talking to me, I can't hear you when I'm in the shower." Zach's words were muffled behind the white and black geometric-patterned shower curtain.

There was no sense in having a conversation with her husband when he couldn't hear her. Besides, she'd asked him the same question as they'd walked away from her parents' house, and then again on their drive home. But even though Zach had given her the same answer every time, she still struggled with their decision.

The sound of the running water stopped, and a few moments later, Zach appeared in his sweatpants and Broncos T-shirt, toweling off his black hair.

"Did you say something while I was showering?"

"I don't like keeping a secret from my family again." Payton hugged the pillow closer.

Zach sat beside her on the bed, the scent of his soap and shampoo familiar and comforting. Laz raised his head for a moment before settling back on the floor, his head resting on his front paws. "We were going to tell them, but when your parents made their announcement, it wasn't the right time."

"I never expected my parents to sell the house." Payton rested her head against Zach's shoulder, savoring the warmth of his embrace as his arm encircled her shoulders.

"I don't know which one of you was more surprised —Johanna, Jillian, or you."

"And to put it on the market during the holidays—"

"People do it—maybe not all the time, but houses do sell. The market is still strong in the Springs, so I imagine your parents will get a good offer pretty quickly."

"I thought *we* were the ones who were changing things up."

"And we are." Zach leaned forward, his gray eyes meeting hers. "You're not having second thoughts, are you?"

"No. I'm excited about the move to England and your opportunity to learn more about woodworking and cabinetmaking." Payton closed her eyes for a moment. Sighed. "But Mom and Dad's decision makes me realize how things will be changing back here while we're overseas."

"We'll be overseas for a year—maybe two. And then—"

"And then we don't know." Payton shrugged away from Zach's embrace. "We might come back to

Colorado, or we might not. We can't see that far ahead yet. The one thing we know right now is God's led us to say yes to this opportunity in England."

Zach straightened but remained close. "I know you're giving up a lot so I can do this, Payton."

"Hey, we do life together. And there's volleyball in England too. I'm doing my research before we leave in June."

"We've got time to figure things out."

"Now we just need to figure out when to tell my family about all of this. I really don't want to wait much longer."

"You're getting together with your sisters for your book club the beginning of December. Why don't you go ahead and tell them then?"

"Tell Jo and Jill but not Mom and Dad?" Payton rose and moved to the bathroom to brush her teeth. "That doesn't seem right."

"Then we'll tell them when we go over to decorate for Christmas—"

"Mom and Dad aren't decorating for Christmas, remember? Realtor's orders." Payton gripped the edge of the sink, fighting against the pressure building up in her chest.

There was more change happening than she'd expected.

"Payton." Zach came up behind her, resting his hands on her shoulders. "We'll figure out the right time to tell the family, okay?"

"Okay." She relaxed against him. "Now I just have to make sure I don't slip up during the book club."

Conversation ceased as they flossed and brushed their teeth, the minty flavor of toothpaste rinsed away with swishes of cold water. Could she spend a morning with her sisters and not mention how she and Zach were moving to England?

Probably. All she needed to do was talk less and listen more.

Payton slipped beneath the blankets and moved closer to Zach, who slid his arm beneath her head. Could she move to England knowing that her family home wouldn't be waiting for her when they came back to the States?

"Are you excited to go see the new house?" Zach's question rumbled beneath her ear.

"Excited? Not really. More curious, I guess. I want to be happy for Mom and Dad. Just like we want them —*everyone*—to be happy for us."

"Exactly." The bed shifted a bit as Zach nodded in agreement.

"I wonder if there'll be any more surprises this Christmas season?"

"Isn't this the season of wonder and surprises?"

"I guess so." Payton rolled over to lay on her back. "It's funny, because we like to think of surprises as fun and exciting, but sometimes they cause things to change. And then you have to choose between holding on to what was and embracing the new. You can't have both. It's like crossing a river . . . what was on the one side wasn't bad. You can't stand in the middle of the river because that's too dangerous. You have to keep moving forward to the other side. To what's waiting for you. You're moving toward the unknown, and you have to pray and hope for all the goodness there."

"That's quite a philosophical way to look at life right now."

"*Hmm.* It just came to me. It's not so much philosophical as trying to work through things so I can accept all the changes." Payton turned her head, able to make out the outline of Zach's profile in the moonlight. "So we tell everyone about England as soon as we can?"

"Yes."

"And we're excited for Mom and Dad."

"Yes."

She'd have to work on that part—transitioning her hesitancy to excitement. Supporting her parents' decision in the same way she and Zach wanted to be supported.

Things were changing more than she'd expected—and possibly more changes were coming. She didn't know. The important thing was to not lose the closeness the family had found in recent years, no matter what happened.

2

*F*our days had passed since we'd announced to the girls that we were selling the house. Now here we sat on Monday evening in the dining room with our Realtor. The china had been put away until next Thanksgiving, which would happen in the new house. The only nod to the upcoming Christmas holiday? The balsam-scented candle I'd lit and placed on the sideboard, a small wreath on the front door, and the Realtor-approved Christmas tree positioned front and center by the living room window.

"How do you both feel? Are you ready for the open house this weekend?" Tracey wrapped her hands around her coffee mug, her bright red nails shining under the dining room light.

"Isn't that your job to tell us? Are we ready?" I handed her a bowl with a brownie and a small scoop of vanilla ice cream. If we were going to talk business, we might as well enjoy some comfort food.

"The house looks fantastic, Heather. I wish all my clients were as thorough as you. No need to call in a stager."

"I appreciate the housecleaning service you recommended. I wasn't looking forward to wiping down baseboards."

"And the Christmas decorations you opted to put up? Perfect."

A tree with white lights and a wreath on the front door. *Fa la la la la.*

"I'll admit I was happy not to climb up a ladder this year and put lights on the house." Don laughed.

"I'm a little sad about not putting our ornaments on the tree—"

"I'm promising Heather we'll get a nice big tree next Christmas in our new house."

"We'll get whatever tree will fit in the house. We're downsizing, remember?"

"Right now, it's not about next year's Christmas tree. It's all about selling this house and moving on to the next big thing waiting for you."

Tracey's words pushed me into the past. *My past.* An echo of my dad's oft-repeated refrain to my mother. *"I found the next big thing, Lou."*

His words always signaled that our lives were about to be turned upside down again. How many times had he disrupted my hopes to stay in a town long enough to make friends? To feel like someone would remember me when we moved on?

I untwisted my fingers, taking my spoon and scooping a bite of warm brownie and cool vanilla ice cream. I savored the perfect comfort food. Selling this house was not a bad decision. We'd stayed here for years—probably longer than we should have. It was past time to move.

Tracey and Don had continued talking. What had I missed?

". . . I'll plan on the open house from ten o'clock to four."

I set my spoon in my bowl. "Isn't that a long time for an open house?"

"Yes, but we're competing with the fact that everyone is Christmas shopping. I want to give people a wide window to come see the house. The closer we get to Christmas and New Year's, the fewer house shoppers will be out there. This is our best weekend."

Don nodded. "You still think putting the house on the market now is a good idea, rather than waiting until the spring?"

"Absolutely—especially since you've already bought your new home. People are still looking and there won't be a lot of homes on the market, which makes your house a hot commodity." She pulled a sheet of paper from her portfolio. "Here's your listing. I've highlighted all the best things about your house. The square footage. The new paint and roof. The new deck. The kitchen isn't as updated as some people will want, but it's large. The bedrooms are all good sized, but most buyers want an en suite with the master bedroom."

It was odd to hear my home being evaluated in such a businesslike manner. The pros and cons. And yet, that was Tracey's job. Potential buyers didn't care that this had been our home since Johanna was two years old. They were considering it for their future home.

And the only way we would decide who bought it would be the bottom line. The best offer.

Selling a house required turning off all my emotions. Ignoring all the memories. That was the only way I could pack up everything, hand the key to someone else, and walk away to start over.

I'd learned how to do that well.

As I took another small bite of dessert, my jaw ached. Tracey had asked if we were ready. We had done so much to prepare for selling this house. We were not changing our minds now.

"Mom? Dad? Where are you?" Johanna's voice sounded from just inside the front door.

"In the dining room."

"There's a car in the driveway." Johanna's footsteps came closer. "Who else is here?"

"Tracey Daniels. Our Realtor."

Johanna stopped beside the table, unbuttoning her tailored black wool coat. "Oh. I didn't realize."

"Hello." Tracey rose, offering Johanna her hand. "It's nice to meet you."

"I'm Johanna, the eldest daughter."

"Yes, I've heard about you—about each of the Thatcher daughters."

"What's going on?" Johanna's gaze lasered in on the paperwork on the table.

"We're discussing the open house that's happening this weekend."

"So soon?" Johanna came and stood between me and her dad.

"As I was just explaining to your parents, this is our best weekend. I'll show the house Saturday and Sunday. The house is already up on the MLS. Your parents have done everything I've asked to make sure it's ready to show."

"How do you feel about that, Mom?"

"We're fine with it. We trust Tracey. She's quite a successful Realtor. If she thinks this is the best thing to do, then we're ready to do it. The house is cleaned and decorated—"

"I saw the substitute Christmas tree set up in front of the living room window."

"It looks nice with the white lights, doesn't it?" Tracey beamed as if she'd strung the white lights on the tree herself.

"It's not our traditional live tree."

"Selling your house during the holidays isn't considered a tradition." Tracey added a professional smile to her response. "The wreath on the front door is perfect too, Heather."

And just like that, our agent had put Johanna, my daughter who was the queen of control, in her place.

Johanna blinked. Looked as if she wanted to say something . . . and then pressed her lips together.

I wanted to apologize. But did I apologize to Tracey? Or to Johanna?

This wasn't about making Johanna happy. This was about doing what we needed to do to sell our house. And I had given up trying to make Johanna happy years ago. That wasn't my responsibility as her mother.

"And what are you listing my parents' house for?"

Johanna was trying to take control again. Typical. Tracey paused, waiting for us to field Johanna's question.

"Johanna, we don't have a problem discussing the sale of our home with you. But right now, we'd like to finish our conversation with Tracey so she can get back to the office—or back home, whichever she needs to do."

Don was calm. Tracey was calm. I was not. I wanted to send Johanna to her room, but she didn't live here anymore. She hadn't in years, not since she'd left for college—and during a few weeks of her pregnancy with Ellison. Selling the house—our house—was not her concern.

Everyone seemed to know that except Johanna.

"I just remembered I have something I need to give

you, Johanna." I stood, wiping my hands on a napkin. "Tracey, why don't you tell Don anything else we need to know—"

"You can always show me whatever it is once you're finished talking, Mom."

"It's fine. I know you need to get home. I assume Ellison is with Beckett." I headed for the kitchen. I could only hope Johanna would follow.

"I'm in no hurry," Johanna continued as the kitchen door closed behind her.

I faced my daughter. "What is going on?"

"What do you mean? You said you had something to give to me."

"That was just a tactic—a rather desperate one—to get you out of the dining room." I brushed my hair off my forehead. "You realize your dad and I can do this on our own, right? We trust Tracey to sell our house."

"Yes, I realize that. Do you think I planned this? I didn't even know she'd be here tonight when I stopped by."

"Why did you stop by?"

Silence.

"Johanna?"

"Why don't you wait until after the New Year to put the house on the market?"

"We told you that we've thought about this for months. We're ready. There's no need to wait."

"The housing market is slow during the holidays—"

"We discussed all this with Tracey. There will still be potential buyers—even some eager to buy. Putting the house on the market now can be like how some businesses do a 'soft' opening. If nothing else, we get feedback about the house and find out if we need to make changes. Improvements. Lower the price. It's still a seller's market. And people do buy houses during the holidays."

"And people wait until after the holidays too."

"But your dad and I decided not to wait." I leaned back against the kitchen counter. "Are you sure there's nothing else bothering you?"

"I'm certain."

"I did need to tell you something—you and Payton and Jillian." I straightened but still couldn't quite meet Johanna eye-to-eye, not with her height. "We need you to clear anything of yours out of the attic. I don't think there's much left, but we might as well do it now before we have an offer on the house."

"Of course. I can tell Jill and Payton."

Johanna's chilly tone conveyed the idea that I'd asked her to come and clean the entire house. She left a few minutes later, her attitude quiet.

And when we said goodnight to Tracey ten minutes later, Johanna still sat in her car in front of the house, her hands gripping the steering wheel, staring straight ahead.

"Should one of us go talk to her?" I stood with Don in the open doorway, the cool air creating little clouds out of my words.

"You know Johanna will talk to us when she's ready —and only then."

"You're right."

Something most definitely was bothering my first-born. Was it the sale of this house—or something else she wasn't telling me?

3

*P*ayton settled the plate filled with fresh blueberry muffins in the middle of the table centered in the breakfast nook of the house she and Zach had purchased in old Colorado Springs. "Let me know what you think."

"Vegan?" Johanna arched a perfectly formed eyebrow.

"Yes." Payton shrugged. "I'm not trying to convert you, Jo. I want to find more recipes Zach and I can both enjoy so we're not eating separate meals all the time. I don't want to always be the 'he eats this and I eat that' couple."

"Then just eat what he eats."

"I've considered it."

"Why do you eat vegan?" Johanna's question was more curious than accusatory.

Payton set the French press in front of Johanna, considering her sister's question as she settled into her chair. "You may pour, big sister. I thought we'd all just enjoy the same coffee today. No Keurig versus French press. I'll add my sugars and Jillian will add her fresh cream."

"What a novel idea."

"As to why I eat vegan . . ." Payton set a muffin on her plate. "I discussed this with a friend of mine who is a counselor, just in a casual sort of way. And I realized it was a way to have control after Pepper died."

"Really?" Jillian moved her mug decorated with a purple columbine closer to Johanna so she could fill it with coffee.

"After Pepper died, I couldn't control a lot of things in my life. I couldn't handle my grief. But I could have a sense of control over what I ate. Over time, I liked eating vegan." Payton added a smear of vegan butter to her muffin. "Now, I'm used to it. Zach and I have talked about whether I would . . . *expand* my dietary options or not. I'm praying about it. He's not pushing me."

"I'm not sure why you have to pray about this—but whatever works for you two, I'm certain you and Zach will figure it out." Johanna cut her muffin in half.

This conversation was an indicator of how her relationship with her sisters had improved in the last two years. They'd *discussed* why she was a vegan, instead of arguing about it. Johanna hadn't confronted her or ridiculed her. And Jillian hadn't needed to step in as the buffer.

Johanna poured the coffee, serving Jillian first and

then Payton, thanking her for making her favorite coffee.

Given the chance, would Payton go through everything she'd experienced in the last few years again? Reconnecting with Zach? Revealing the secret about the night Pepper died? Her stumbling journey of faith?

Yes.

This hard-fought relationship with her sisters was worth it. And marrying Zach had been one of the best surprises—the best blessing.

"Today couldn't have come at a better time." While avoiding one topic, Payton decided to broach the issue she knew her sisters had to be thinking about as much as she was.

"Something tells me we're not discussing a book today." Jillian brushed muffin crumbs from her fingertips.

"Surprise." Payton shared a smile with her sisters. "Did either of you even bring a book? Good thing we renamed this group the 'Coffee and Maybe a Book Club.'"

Johanna's smile mirrored Payton's. "No sense in fighting the reality of our monthly Saturday mornings."

"So . . . Mom and Dad." Payton glanced at both her sisters. "Were either of you as shocked as I was with their decision to sell the house? And now they're having an open house while we're sitting here drinking coffee."

Johanna set her cup down. "They didn't even talk to us first."

"They don't have to talk to us first, Joey." Jillian sipped her coffee. "We don't talk to them about our major life decisions."

Payton gave a silent cheer after Jillian stepped up to the plate and took a bold verbal swing like that.

"This decision affects all of us."

"In a way, yes." Jillian continued to handle their older sister's arguments. "But what are we going to do? Tell them they shouldn't have bought a house? Storm the open house and tell them not to sell the house?"

"Mom and Dad aren't that old—I mean, Dad's seventy-one, right? Why are they talking about downsizing?"

"Why do they need to wait? They did a lot of cleaning and organizing during COVID—"

"A lot of people did."

"Maybe they just realized the house is too big for them." Payton swallowed a sip of rich, sweet coffee, deciding it was time to help Jillian. "It is just the two of them in that big house."

"It's our home . . . *their* home." Johanna corrected her slipup. "And it isn't a mansion, Payton. They've been happy there for years."

"And now they're not."

Trying to figure out how their parents made their decisions was no easier than trying to read their minds.

Jillian had shredded her muffin into pieces.

Maybe it was foolish to have started this discussion.

But if she hadn't asked the question, Jillian or Johanna would have.

"Where did they say the new house is?"

Jillian reached for another muffin—to eat or to shred, Payton could only guess. "The Briargate area, I believe."

"I talked to Mom midweek and found the listing." Johanna pulled out her iPad. "I'm just thankful they didn't buy anything in Monument. I wouldn't want them dealing with all that snow."

It was no surprise to Payton that Johanna had done her research on the house. That's what Johanna did— focused on the facts. "Does it have a decent yard? Dad always loved yard work."

"A small one with a small deck." Johanna set the iPad in the middle of the table, but neither Payton nor Jillian picked it up.

Johanna had gone ahead and talked with their parents—gathering more intel like she always did. She was less of a control freak these days, but she still preferred to be involved with what was going on. Very involved.

"Maybe Mom and Dad want to travel more." Jillian added more coffee to her cup, offering some to both Johanna and Payton. "They can do more of that now that Mom's not working and Dad's only doing some occasional consulting."

"I wonder how she feels about that adjustment?" Johanna sipped her coffee. "Do you think that's why they started looking at houses? Were they bored?"

"Mom never complains." Payton offered more muffins to her sisters, but they both declined. "It has to help that they'd paid the house off."

"All the more reason for them to stay in the house." Johanna seemed ready to go rehash the decision to move with her parents.

"Well, Mom and Dad have already made up their minds, haven't they?" Payton tried to keep her voice low, calm. To sound like Mom.

"I'm just glad that it looks like the agent didn't talk them into spending more than they should have on that new house." Johanna again.

"Stop snooping around in Mom and Dad's finances, Jo." Payton forced herself to speak calmly. "Mom and Dad are adults, remember? They're not going to be duped by a Realtor."

Payton had eaten her muffin without tasting a single bite. What a waste of her time and effort.

What was the real reason her parents' decision bothered her? She'd wrestled with the truth all week. Didn't want to admit it—not even to Zach, who'd commented last night on how quiet she was.

"Are you nervous about the book club tomorrow with your sisters? Afraid you'll mention our move to England?"

"No. If I focus the conversation on Mom and Dad and their house, everything will be fine."

Payton stuffed a bit of muffin in her mouth. Chewed. Dumped an unneeded fourth spoonful of sugar into her coffee, all the while realizing she was delaying.

"It's the memories."

"What?" Johanna's gaze landed on her.

Payton raised her voice. "It's the memories."

"Payton's right." Jillian set her coffee cup on the table.

"We all grew up in that house." Payton swallowed against the sharp bite of tears in the back of her throat. "Mom came from the hospital after Pepper and I were born . . . to that house."

Jillian's mouth twisted. Johanna sat silent, unblinking.

"That house was your safe place when you were pregnant, Johanna." Payton gripped her hands together beneath the table, willing herself not to cry. "I know you didn't want to move back home with Mom and Dad, but at least you knew you could. You knew they were there to take care of you when you were on bed rest."

"True." One short word of affirmation.

"We don't lose the memories if . . . *when* Mom and Dad sell the house." Again, Jillian spoke needed truth.

"It feels like we do." This was the reality Payton had carried around ever since Mom and Dad had made their announcement.

"I know. I don't like it, and the first few birthdays and holidays will feel odd, but—"

"I can't talk about this." Johanna stood. "I appreciate all your insights. Your maturity. But I-I can't even think about strangers walking through our home."

And with that, Johanna paced to the front door,

gathered her coat and purse, and left, a gust of December air entering the house as the door opened and closed.

It was as if Mrs. All Is Calm had turned into the Abominable Snowwoman.

Her older sister's voice had cracked. Wobbled.

Was the house somehow more important to Johanna than to Jillian? To her?

"What did I miss, Jill?"

"I have no idea. Do you think she's upset Mom didn't ask for her advice? Mom always checks with Joey about things like what chair cushions to buy or when to get new curtains. And now she bought an entire house without talking to her."

"You're saying she's jealous of the Realtor?"

Jillian raised her hands, palms up. "Maybe."

"Should we talk to Mom? Ask her to consult Johanna on a few decisions?"

Jillian collapsed against her chair, her shoulders slumped. "What do you think Johanna would do if she found out we meddled like that?"

"You're right. Bad idea."

"Are you okay with Mom and Dad selling the house?"

"I will be . . . eventually. Hopefully by the time they close." Payton stood, gathering the paper napkins, but remained by the table. "Right now? I'm sad. It's such an unexpected change in the midst of the holiday season. Zach's busy with some big projects and I'm gearing up for volleyball club season."

Not that she could tell Jillian it would be her last
season with Club Brio.

"I don't know if there would ever be a good time for
Mom and Dad to make this decision. Would we ever be
ready?"

"That's a good point. How are you feeling about all
this, Jill?"

"Well—" Jillian laughed, the sound sharp and
short. "On Thanksgiving, Geoff and I were going to tell
everyone we were thinking of visiting his brother Brian
and his family this Christmas."

"What?" Payton wasn't the only Thatcher sister
whose announcement had been delayed by Mom and
Dad's "we bought a house and we're moving"
declaration.

"We were just considering it. But after Mom and
Dad's news, we decided this isn't the right time."

"Oh, Jill, I'm sorry."

"The good news is, things have improved so much
with Geoff and Brian, he wants to go visit his brother."

"We've been praying about that for months."

Jill picked up the plate of muffins, following Payton
to the sink, where she dumped out the remnants of
Johanna's coffee. "I know. Maybe we'll go in the spring.
The best thing we can do right now is pray for Mom
and Dad while they sell the house."

"And for Johanna—and whatever is bothering her."

Once again, Payton and Jillian were aligning them-
selves. Johanna would say they were opposing her. But
she was wrong. They might believe different things

about God, but when Payton and Jillian prayed for Johanna, they were *for* Johanna, not against her.

The tightness in Payton's chest eased. "We'll have some prayer time before you go home, okay?"

Jillian leaned in for a hug. "I was thinking the same thing. And let's pray about tomorrow too."

"Tomorrow?"

"I promised to take Mom Christmas shopping during the open house. Dad's working on some secret Christmas project."

"Ooh—surprises. Sounds like fun."

"I'm not one for crowds, but if it helps Dad surprise Mom, it'll be worth it."

"It's almost time for bed, Ellison." Johanna retrieved a stray shoe from underneath the coffee table, grabbing a red plastic block and a small stuffed sloth hidden there too.

People would think she never cleaned her house. Or that she lived with a toddler who was bent on destroying any sense of order in her life. The evergreen scent of the live tree decorated with multicolored lights and ornaments tucked safely in a corner corralled behind a plastic baby gate, away from her daughter's curious fingers, added a bit of holiday cheer.

Ellison's only response was another burst of giggles as she and Beckett rolled on the living room floor,

Beckett holding her close and tickling her through her penguin footie pajamas.

Johanna sidestepped Beckett's body. "Almost bedtime, I said."

"Yes, Mommy." Beckett's tone was a high singsong, his dark eyes glinting.

"I am not your mommy."

"I am well aware of that." Beckett righted himself, settling Ellison in his lap. "Tell Mommy yes, sweetheart."

"Yes." Ellison pushed her hair out of her face.

"Daddy will read you some books first, okay?"

Ellison wrapped her arms around Beckett's neck as Beckett rose to his feet. "Book, Mommy?"

"Daddy will read to you tonight. Mommy has to clean the kitchen—"

"Sit with us, Johanna." Beckett held his hand out. "It won't take that long. And then we'll both clean up the dinner dishes."

Fine.

She gathered two Christmas-themed books—only two—from the basket beside the couch, settling next to Beckett, while Ellison snuggled on his lap. The fragrance of her daughter's lavender lotion intertwined with his aftershave. This had become one of her favorite aromas.

Beckett took full advantage of story time, doing woodland animal voices and faces that made both Ellison and Johanna laugh. When he wasn't there in the evening, which was more and more infrequent, Johanna's book reading paled in comparison.

When he was done reading *Bear Stays Up for Christmas*, Beckett announced, "I'll tuck her in."

"I know." Johanna kissed her daughter's forehead. "Sleep well."

"'Night, Mommy."

Ten minutes later, Beckett joined her in the kitchen.

"You spoil her, you know, rocking her to sleep."

"It's a father's prerogative to spoil his daughter." Beckett nudged her away from the sink. "I'll finish loading the dishwasher."

"I'm okay with that. Do you want some dessert?"

"Is there any ice cream left?"

"I bought several pints of Ben & Jerry's Phish Food earlier this week."

"My favorite."

"Why do you think I bought it?"

While he finished with the dinner dishes, she prepped their dessert.

"Your parents' decision to buy a new house got me thinking." Beckett took the bowl she offered him and followed her back to the couch.

"About what?" She settled on the couch lengthwise, resting her feet in Beckett's lap.

"About buying a house."

"Why would you buy a house?"

"The lease on my apartment ends in a couple of

months. It's a good time to buy a house instead of
continuing to rent."

"True."

"And I was thinking I . . . we . . . we could look for
something for the three of us."

Johanna dropped her spoon into her bowl with a
sharp clatter of metal against ceramic. "*What?*"

"It makes sense. I've been paying rent on an apartment. You're paying a mortgage. Why don't we just buy
a house together—"

"And live together?"

"Well, of course. I think Ellison would like it if her
parents lived together, don't you?"

Johanna jerked away, planting her feet on the floor.
"Don't bring Ellison into this, Beckett."

"Ellison is very much a part of this decision. She
has a mother and a father who don't live together—"

"She's not the only child dealing with that—"

"I'd like to change the situation before she does
have to *deal* with it."

"The agreement we have is working fine." Johanna
set her bowl on the coffee table, wiping her hands with
her napkin.

Be calm.

"Will you just listen to me for a minute?" Beckett
mirrored her movements, turning to face her. "Things
are great, Johanna. Great. Okay? I love living in
Colorado. I love my job. Ellison is wonderful. I love my
daughter more than I ever thought possible. And I love
you—you have to know that."

Johanna refused to react to Beckett's words, the ones where she ranked fourth behind Colorado, his job, and their daughter.

"I should have expected this. Expected you would want more than our original arrangement. It's because I've slipped up and let you stay over—"

Beckett growled low in his throat. "This is not about how we've *slipped up* and slept together again. Johanna, we've been together for a decade. And don't —*don't* throw my past transgression in my face, please."

"I still think about it . . . sometimes . . ." She hated admitting it, the words forced out against her will.

"I can't undo the past. Am I going to spend the rest of my life waiting for you to forgive me, completely forgive me, for how I hurt you?"

"I don't know." Johanna stood, putting space between them, releasing and redoing her ponytail with sharp jerks of her hair. "I'm . . . I'm happy with the way things are."

"But I'm not. And one day, our daughter is going to ask us why we don't live together. Can't we give her a complete family, one where we live in the same house?"

Johanna bent to retrieve one of Ellison's little socks from underneath the coffee table. How had she missed it when she was picking up earlier? Where was its mate?

"Johanna?"

"I wasn't expecting this. Ellison's happy here. This

is the only home she's known. I brought her here right from the hospital."

"I remember—I had that ridiculous stuffed giraffe waiting for her." Beckett paused for a moment, as if giving Johanna time to say anything else. "I'm not trying to make things worse for us. I see this—buying a house together—as a good thing."

"I know you do."

Beckett was a good man—he'd proven that over and over since Ellison's birth. Agreeing to all her conditions about their parenting arrangement. Helping on short notice when Johanna's schedule at the hospital pharmacy demanded it. He'd never given her any reason to doubt his loyalty to their daughter or to her. Still, his one infidelity haunted her at times.

He came and stood close—but not too close. "Maybe we can talk about this again in a few weeks?"

"Okay."

"I'm thinking it's probably a good idea if I head back to my place tonight." Beckett tucked his hands in his jean pockets.

"Probably."

"Is it okay if I still meet you and Ellison at the mall tomorrow so she can see Santa?"

"Ellison is expecting you to be there."

"I don't want to disappoint her."

"I know you don't."

"I don't want to disappoint you either, Jo." Beckett's voice was husky.

"I-I know you don't."

After Beckett left, Johanna stood outside Ellison's bedroom door, imagined her tucked beneath her blankets, sound asleep.

All's right with the world.

She'd omit the line Robert Browning had penned about "God's in His heaven" because, well, that wasn't what made things right in her world. Or Ellison's. God was fine for Payton and Jillian. She no longer wanted to fight her sisters about their faith.

But one day Ellison would grow up and learn that all wasn't right with the world—just like Johanna had. No matter how much she wanted to protect her daughter from that reality, she couldn't.

Johanna sighed, leaning her forehead against the closed bedroom door.

Why had she resisted Beckett's suggestion they buy a house together? Was it because of his past? Their past?

Or was it because she wanted more from him than what he was offering her?

4

*J*illian had attended church service last night, enjoying the blend of contemporary worship songs with traditional Christmas music, so she could spend time with Mom today. As expected, the open-air mall was busy, the sidewalks crowded with shoppers, the stores decorated for the holidays, the winter air filled with nonstop music.

"There's one advantage to putting the house on the market." Mom's words came from behind as they exited White House Black Market.

"What's that?" Jillian held opened the door, allowing another woman humming "We Wish You a Merry Christmas" along with the piped-in music to enter the store after Mom followed her outside.

"I'm getting my Christmas shopping done earlier than usual." Mom raised her arms to display several shopping bags. "Johanna is going to love those black pants for work—and they were on sale too."

"Am I ever going to convince you of the convenience of online shopping, Mom?"

"Oh, I do some of that too. But I enjoy getting out and shopping for some of my Christmas presents. The decorations, the excitement . . ."

"No parking, the long lines . . . which is why I enjoy adding my purchases to a virtual shopping cart and then opening my front door a few days later and retrieving the boxes waiting for me."

"Do you remember when your dad would watch you and your sisters one Saturday in December so I could go shopping all day?" Mom smiled at the memory, small laugh lines appearing at the corners of her eyes.

"Yes. You always made sure we baked sugar cookies the night before so we could decorate them and then eat them while you were gone." The memory warmed Jillian like a hug as they passed the storefronts filled with displays decorated with fake ornaments and snow. "And if it snowed, which it did once or twice, Dad would help us build snowmen or snow forts."

"Our neighbors loved seeing the Thatcher girls' snow families all decked out with scarves and hats and carrot noses."

"The deer enjoyed those carrot noses too."

"We always had replacement carrots for noses."

Time with her mom, sharing memories, was its own special gift.

The more gifts Mom bought, the broader her smile. They'd spent a good part of the morning discussing gift options for Ellison. Had she ever realized how much Mom loved Christmas?

It made Jillian love the season all the more.

"Shall we take these bags to the car and come back for another round of shopping? Or head north to Castle Rock?" Jillian paused at the crosswalk to allow a car to pass. "Or are you hungry?"

"So many choices. I'd like to check out the cooking store before we head anywhere else. They might have something there I can add to your dad's grilling tools." Mom nodded toward the direction of the parking lot and Jillian's car. "But I'm also hungry and ready to eat. You?"

"Let's eat then."

Their attempt to make a beeline to her car became a dance of dodging other shoppers, but finally they locked their purchases in the car and decided to have lunch at P.F. Chang's. The warmth of the restaurant invited them to slip off their gloves and coats and relax against the booth.

"Where did you say Dad is today while Tracey hosts the second day of the open house?" Jillian accepted the menu from the waitress.

"I couldn't tell you. He's very secretive all of a sudden. He told me to have fun, not to max out the credit card"—Mom laughed—"and then he *ho-ho-ho*ed as he headed to his car."

"Is Dad moonlighting as Santa Claus?"

"I don't think so." Mom paused while the waitress brought them glasses of water and then took their orders. "We're both out of the house, per Tracey's instructions."

"Interesting."

"You'd tell me if you knew what your dad was up to, right?"

"Of course—unless it was a fun Christmas surprise and I was sworn to secrecy." Jillian grinned. "But honestly, Mom, I don't know what Dad's doing today."

Mom's innocent question was a reminder of how their family had learned the importance of not keeping secrets from one another. A surprise was harmless. Fun. A secret? That could be devastating.

Instrumental Christmas music wove its way through the restaurant. The soundtrack of the season promised a magical, harmonious time of year.

But no one was guaranteed peace and goodwill and joy, even if it was the holiday season.

"How are you and Geoff doing?" Mom squeezed a wedge of lemon in her water.

"Are you asking in general? Or do you want a specific answer?"

"I don't want to pry, Jill. Any way you want to answer."

"We're good. Really. His job is going well. I'm happy to be home—happier than I've been in a while."

And that was her "in general" answer.

"We were considering going to visit his brother and his family for Christmas, but . . ."

Mom unfolded her napkin and arranged her silver-ware on the table with a soft metallic clink. "But?"

"After you and Dad told us you were putting the house on the market, we decided to postpone the trip until the spring."

"Oh, Jill, you should go if that's what you want to do."

"I don't want to—not if this is the last Christmas at home." Jillian kept any hint of disappointment from her voice. Life was about adjustments—if anyone had learned that lesson, she had. "And I knew you might need help with things—like cleaning the attic. We're fine."

"Well, I hope you go in the spring, then, whether we've sold the house by then or not."

Jillian sipped her ice water, appreciating how it soothed her dry mouth as she considered broaching the anything-but-general next topic. "We're also discussing the topic of . . . of children again."

Mom's hazel eyes widened, but she remained silent, waiting until the waitress delivered their order of Mongolian beef and sweet and sour chicken before she spoke. "You are?"

"We agreed to not talk about children for two years. It's time to put the topic back on the table." She trans-ferred brown rice to her plate. "I don't know what we'll decide, but back when we tabled the conversation, we said we'd get the help of a professional counselor if we needed to."

"An objective viewpoint?"

"That's what we're hoping for. We've had a lot of fun the last two years, doing the additional renovation on the house, and hiking, and giving me time to adjust to not working full-time at the bank anymore. But it's time to tackle the tough topic now."

Discussing this with Mom made it all the more real. Like mixing the words and pouring them out so they set in concrete.

Jillian thought of the Bible verse she'd prayed with Payton for months—the one she'd clung to whenever peace evaded her. How God would give her peace when she focused her thoughts on Him.

This wasn't about her being right and Geoff being wrong. This was about them finding common ground, just like Harper, her best friend, had told her months ago. Figuring out what their family was going to be in the future—even if it was just the two of them.

But she couldn't deny she still wanted to expand their family to include at least one child.

Mom's phone buzzed.

"Oh, this is Tracey. She probably wants to update me about the open house. Do you mind if I answer?"

"Of course not."

Mom eased out of the booth and moved toward the front of the restaurant, giving Jillian time to scan her texts, including a brief one from Geoff.

My parents want to know when we want to do Christmas with them.

How to respond?

While their relationship with his brother,

Brian, had improved, their relationship with his parents was stagnant. There was no changing his mom or his dad—and their interactions were stilted. Formal.

Can't we just do New Year's with them?

She pushed Send as Mom returned to the table and slipped her phone back into her purse. "Everything okay?"

"I guess so." Mom shook her head, offering her a dazed smile. "Yes. Everything is most definitely okay."

"What did your agent say?"

"We have a cash offer on the house."

Jillian's bite of chicken stuck in her throat, causing her to cough. Mom might as well have told her that her dad was the real Santa Claus.

She should be happy—*ecstatic*—for her parents. But all she wanted to say was *"Turn the offer down."*

"Cash?" Jillian coughed again, trying to clear her airway. "Is it a good offer?"

"Apparently. *It's cash,* Jillian. Tracey didn't want to discuss specifics until she could talk to your dad and me together. She's calling him now and wants to meet with us both in her office later."

"Do you want the waitress to pack up our food?"

"No. No, we have plenty of time to eat." Mom speared a piece of beef, as if to prove her intention to relax and eat lunch. "She's going to call me back after she talks to your dad and tell me what time we're meeting. When I said I was with you, Tracey said she'd call him."

"This is fantastic, Mom!" Jillian clasped her mom's hand. "Aren't you excited?"

"I guess so." Mom gave her head a little shake, as if bemused by the reality. "I'm more surprised than anything."

It was as if someone pushed the fast-forward button and suddenly Christmas was only a few days away. Time was moving too quickly. Jillian hadn't expected her parents' house to sell this weekend—certainly no one in the family had expected this.

What would Johanna and Payton say?

Jillian's chest burned, killing her appetite.

It was only a house. It shouldn't matter this much.

But it did.

MY PHONE RANG AGAIN.

"This must be Tracey." I glanced at my phone. "No, wait. It's your dad."

Jillian motioned for me to take the call.

"Don, did Tracey—"

"It's Zach—"

"Zach?"

My one-word question snared Jillian's attention.

"Dad's been with me this morning . . . working on a project . . . but he collapsed." Despite Zach's calm tone, his words acted like a jolt of electricity through me. "I called 911. He's on his way to the hospital—Payton is with him in the ambulance."

I struggled to process everything Zach had told me, but his words seemed scrambled. *Collapsed. Ambulance.* "Wh-what's wrong?"

"They're not sure. His heart rate was too low when the EMTs checked it. He got a gash on his head when he fell, but that's a minor concern. I'm heading to the hospital now. Do you want me to pick you up and bring you to the hospital?"

"No. No, I'm with Jill. She can drive me. Do I need to call Johanna?"

"Yes—at least I think so. Payton was focused on Dad."

"I'll call her while Jill drives."

Zach's phone call was like a tornado appearing out of nowhere and upending the day. If we walked out of the restaurant and saw cars overturned and roofs torn off buildings, I wouldn't be surprised.

Zach had ended the phone call, but I still gripped the phone so hard my fingers ached.

I didn't care about a cash offer on our house.

I didn't care about Christmas.

I wanted my husband to be okay.

"Mom? Mom?" Jillian's hand touched mine, easing my phone from my fingers. "Tell me what's going on."

"Your dad . . . he's on the way to the hospital."

"What happened?" As her face paled, Jill's voice remained even, an echo of Zach's calmness.

How could they both stay so composed?

"He was with Zach . . . I don't know . . . he collapsed . . . Zach called 911 . . . Payton is with your dad in the ambulance . . ." I stood up. "We need to go—"

Jill caught my arm, pulling me back down to sit in the booth. "Mom, I'm handling it."

The waitress appeared, our food bagged, offering Jill the black rectangular folder with the bill.

"Wait. I was paying for lunch . . ."

"I'm handling it." Jill softened her words with a smile. "If you want to use the restroom before we leave, go ahead."

"I'm fine."

No. No, I wasn't.

I'd switched roles with my daughter, allowing her to take care of me. She'd started while I was still on the phone.

I remained still as Jill paid the check. The restaurant seemed quiet, as if we were in a soundproof booth, cut off from the holiday hustle and bustle.

Hurry up.

No. Slow down. Don't panic.

I repeated *Don't panic* to myself like a mantra all the way to the car, thankful Jillian had driven today.

"Which hospital, Mom?"

"What?" My hands shook so much I couldn't work the seat belt.

"Which hospital are they taking Dad to?"

"I don't know. I forgot to ask." Or had Zach told me and I couldn't remember? "Let me call Zach."

"I'll call Zach. Then I'll call Johanna."

"We need to get to the hospital."

"But to do that, we have to know which hospital." She paused. "Wait, Mom, Zach already texted me. Penrose-St. Francis."

"Fine."

"Just sit back and try to relax. I'll call Jo while I drive."

I gripped the door handle as Jill backed out of the parking space. Outside, people strolled along the sidewalk. Laughing. Talking. Sipping coffee in insulated cups. Carrying bags filled with presents. Families. Friends. Doing normal things, uninterrupted by an emergency.

The phone call had fractured the day, reminding me once again how quickly my good life could be disrupted. How useless it was to think I could relax . . . could believe life was really good at last.

The force of Zach's words pressed down on my chest. My heart. I couldn't breathe. Maybe I needed to lean over and rest my head on my knees until the light-headedness passed. But the seat belt held me in place.

I needed to stay upright. Couldn't . . . wouldn't fall apart.

". . . we're on our way to the hospital now. Payton is with Dad." Jill was speaking to Johanna. "We should be there in less than ten minutes."

"Is she coming?"

Jill ignored my question.

"Fine. Dad and Mom were supposed to meet with their Realtor later, but I'll call and cancel that."

Tracey.

I needed to call Tracey. But I remained frozen, my cell phone clasped in my hands.

Jill ended the call, navigating the car out of the parking lot and east onto Briargate Parkway before speaking to me. The heavy gray clouds overhead indicated possible snow later.

"Jo and Beckett are going to meet us at the hospital."

"What about Ellison?"

"I imagine Ellison will be with them or they'll find someone to watch her."

"I need to call Tracey back."

"Just dial her number, Mom, and put it on speaker. I'll talk to her."

It was easier to do what Jillian wanted than to insist on doing things my way.

"This is Tracey Daniels."

Jill spoke before I could even say hello.

"Tracey, this is Heather and Don Thatcher's daughter Jillian."

"Oh . . . Hello. Is everything okay?"

"Actually, no . . . no, it's not." Jillian paused, swallowing hard. "My father collapsed an hour or so ago— I'm not sure of all the details. He's being taken to the hospital by ambulance. I'm taking my mother there now."

"I'm so sorry—"

"Thank you." Jillian accepted Tracey's response with kindness but focused on what needed to be said.

"Obviously, my parents won't be able to meet with you to discuss the cash offer on their house."

"Of course not. Tell them not to worry. I'll talk to the buyers and let them know we'll contact them in the next day or two."

I needed to say something—be part of the conversation. "Thank you, Tracey."

"Oh, Heather—I didn't know you were listening. I'm so sorry about Don. Please, don't worry about anything. We'll talk soon. My thoughts and best wishes are with you and Don."

Tracey was echoing my own thoughts that were on rewind.

Please, let Don be okay. Please, let Don be okay. Please, let Don be okay.

But I'd learned again and again that wishing and hoping for something didn't make it happen.

The aroma of Chinese food filled the car, nauseating me. I needed to get to the hospital. But how was I going to walk in and face . . . what, I didn't know.

"Do you want me to drop you off at the ER entrance?" Jillian turned into the parking lot.

"Yes. No. Just . . . just park and we'll walk in together."

"Fine. I didn't want you to walk in by yourself."

Jillian pulled into a vacant slot as I scanned the area. Stopped. I was avoiding looking at the ER entrance. "Do you think your dad and Zach are already here?"

"Probably." As Jillian and I got out of her car, she

came and linked her arm through mine. "We'll get through this, Mom. I'm praying."

The sharp wail of a siren pierced the air as an ambulance pulled away from the emergency room. Someone else's life upended in a moment—but help was on the way. Would it be in time? Would it be enough?

I'd faced death . . . loss . . . before in a hospital. Pepper's death didn't exempt me from losing my husband. That's not how life worked.

"Keep praying, Jilly. Keep praying."

I don't know if her prayers counted for me since I'd never believed in God. Believe in some heavenly father when your own father didn't care about you?

No, thank you.

a lone with my husband at last.

Of course, Don rested with his eyes closed in a semi-reclining hospital bed, while I sat in the typical hard plastic chair pulled up alongside, not that I was complaining. A bandage covered the two stitches he'd needed for the small gash in his forehead. A nurse entered and exited the room at various intervals, always with a brief hello, a candy-cane-striped stethoscope cover adding a bit of cheer to her efficient manner. At one point, she'd turned on the television, tuning it to a cooking show, the volume on low.

The family had believed me—finally—when I'd assured them that I was fine, completely fine. Johanna had abandoned the idea she was the one who needed to stay overnight with her dad. I'd needed to remind her that she'd promised Ellison she would come in and kiss her goodnight. I'd allowed her to get me one last bottle of water from the cafeteria, and she'd added an apple and a small salad, instructing me to eat as she'd hugged me goodbye.

I rested my hand on top of Don's where it lay on the blanket, thankful his IV was in his other arm. I couldn't help wondering if I'd be up all night watching one cooking show after the other.

"I'm not asleep." Don's voice was a low rumble.

"I wasn't sure."

"You know, this wasn't what I had planned for today."

His words pulled a laugh from me, past the ache that had lodged in my chest ever since Zach's phone call. At last, a little humor after a frantic, fearful rush to the hospital and hours in the ER. And uncertainty. Still, the uncertainty.

"Really? Collapsing and taking a ride in an ambulance with Payton wasn't anywhere on your schedule when you woke up and planned out your day?"

"Not even penciled in." Don shifted in the bed. "I'm sorry I scared everyone."

"You've said that a dozen times, Don. We're all scared because we love you. And you're not a fainter." I'd try to keep up the lighthearted tone.

"When is that doctor going to come in and talk to us?"

"Going somewhere, are you?" I pointed to the monitors clustered at the head of his bed creating a medical cacophony of hums and beeps, one of them spitting out a long strip of paper. "Dragging your IV with you?"

"I guess I should be glad I'm only doing consulting work—no need to worry about calling the boss."

"Retirement does simplify things." We shared a smile. "Jillian called Tracey, who has explained to our interested buyer that there's a short delay in our responding to their offer."

"You want to take it, right?"

"A cash offer? Why wouldn't we?" I adjusted my hold on Don's hand as he laced his fingers through mine. "But we need to sit down with Tracey and discuss things like when we want to close. I never imagined we'd get an offer so quickly—"

The door to the room opened and the cardiologist we'd met earlier in the ER entered with a "good evening," motioning me to remain sitting. Don tried to push himself up to a sitting position as the doctor came to stand by the bed.

"You stay comfortable, Mr. Thatcher—as comfortable as you can be with all that paraphernalia."

"Can't say I'm overly fond of the big sticky things on my chest."

"I'm Dr. Gossert, by the way. We met earlier in the day, but then you've had quite a busy day, haven't you? Those 'sticky things' are external pacer pads. You need those in case you should go into a prolonged period of asystole—no heartbeat—so we can hook these up to a pacer generator and get your heart beating again."

"Then I guess I have no complaints about them, do I?"

And now I gripped my husband's hand. Hard. "Is there a danger of that?"

"To be completely frank—yes." Dr. Gossert focused on Don. "Your heartbeat is low, irregular. We're doing further tests to rule out a heart attack, even though we're fairly certain that's not the issue."

As the cardiologist talked, the ache in my chest returned.

"What do you think is the problem?" Don asked the question before I had a chance.

"We think we're dealing with tachycardia-brady-cardia syndrome—tachy-brady, for short. It means that you have episodes of very slow heartbeats and then episodes of very fast heart rates. We've seen some of those while we've been monitoring you." He nodded toward the machines. "I can show them to you before I leave. Have you been lightheaded in recent months or weeks? Short of breath? Any chest pains?"

"As I said in the ER, nothing that I thought was worth mentioning to my doctor. I get tired at times during the day, but I'm not in my twenties anymore. I've had some lightheadedness, but that happens to everyone. How did I get this?"

"The risk for tachy-brady does increase with age, but it can also be caused by some stress on the heart or by an injury to your body's natural pacemaker, such as a heart attack or a viral illness—even sleep apnea. That's why we're doing additional tests."

I zeroed in on some of the doctor's words. "Don was

diagnosed with sleep apnea several years ago, but he didn't like wearing the apparatus at night."

"Who would?" A defensive note crept into Don's voice.

"Another cardiac electrophysiologist will be in tomorrow to discuss the option of a pacemaker to regulate your heartbeat and not let it drop so low that you faint again."

"A pacemaker?" I pressed my hand over my mouth, wishing my question sounded calmer. How did we get to the point of discussing a pacemaker?

"She'll explain more, but it's a relatively straightforward procedure we can do here in the hospital. You stay overnight for the monitoring and then go home the next day."

"Sounds like we'll have this figured out within the next twenty-four hours?"

"Most likely, unless we uncover another issue." Dr. Gossert moved to the monitors, explaining the black squiggles on the strip of paper denoting where Don's heart had slowed down and then sped up again. "Any other questions?"

"Not right now. Heather?"

"No. Thank you for taking so much time with us."

"Your husband is safe, Mrs. Thatcher. He's being monitored, as you can see, and an alarm will go off if his heartbeat gets too low. You can go home to sleep—"

"I plan on staying here."

"That's fine, too, although your bed will be more comfortable than the recliner."

"Understood—but I won't sleep any better at home."

Once the cardiologist left, I settled back in the chair beside Don's bed.

"It's fine for you to go home, Heather." Don rested his head against the pillow. "You just might sleep better in our bed."

"Do you want me to go home?"

"No." He reached for my hand again. "I'd miss you."

"I'd miss you too. After forty-three years of marriage, I'm used to being with you. Jillian ran home and got me a toothbrush and some other things, including my pillow and a blanket. She even brought your Broncos blanket." That earned a smile from my husband. "I'll be fine right over there in the recliner. It's only one night."

"Or maybe two or three, if I get a pacemaker."

"I'll manage—I'll just have to stake my claim with Johanna." I waved the remote. "And I'm in charge of this."

Don shook his head, but his smile never wavered. "You are taking advantage of a sick man."

"What? You don't want to watch cooking shows with me?"

"I'd rather watch football."

"If I could find you a football game to watch, I would."

"I know you would." He offered me a sly grin. "What if I can find a replay?"

"Don, you know how I feel about watching replays of football games."

"Just this once?"

"Okay. I'll indulge you—just this once." My husband knew I was lying. If he wanted to watch replays of football all night long, I'd do it without a single complaint.

6

*P*ayton stomped her feet as she stood outside her parents' front door, shaking the dampness from her shoes. Snow had started falling as she left her house twenty minutes ago, a casual kind of snow that dusted the grass and trees but only dampened the roads and grayed the skies.

Before she could even search out the spare key from her purse, the door swung open, causing the simple Christmas wreath decorated with pinecones and red berries and a white bow to sway.

"Good morning, Payton."

"Johanna?" Payton gripped her purse to stop from dropping it. "Why are you at Mom and Dad's? It's barely nine o'clock in the morning."

"I could ask you the same thing."

"Mom asked me to come by and pick up a few things for her in case Dad has to stay another night—"

Johanna stiffened. "Dad has to stay another night? Why?"

"Johanna—I said *in case* Dad has to stay another night. Nothing's been decided. They're still waiting for another cardiologist to come and talk to them." Payton stepped into the house, unbuttoning her coat as she toed off her shoes.

"Mom must think there's a good chance Dad's going to be in the hospital longer or she wouldn't have asked you to come get her anything."

"Or maybe she just wants a fresh change of clothes." Payton refused to get caught up in Johanna's rush of tension. "So why are you here?"

"Their house is on the market. I wanted to make certain it looks good in case someone wanted to see it."

"They have an offer on the house—"

"Yes, but you don't take the house off the market until it's a done deal."

"Fine. You're right." Payton left her coat, purse, and shoes in the foyer. "But no one's been here since yesterday. I'm surprised you're not at the hospital visiting Dad."

"I wanted to go, but when I called, Mom told me not to come."

"She did?"

"Like you said, they're waiting for some other doctor to come talk to them and tell them what's next. There was no need for me to go there yet. I needed to do something."

"Shouldn't you be at work?"

"I spoke with Axton and took some emergency leave."

Talking with Johanna was like having a conversation with a toddler who never stopped moving. She checked the fresh flower arrangement of red and white carnations mixed with evergreen boughs on the breakfast nook table, removing a few limp blooms and throwing them in the trash can. Wiped down the spotless countertop. Rearranged the apples and oranges in the ceramic fruit bowl.

All the time, she kept glancing at her phone, as if willing it to ring. Wanting Mom to call and update her on Dad.

For once, Payton understood exactly how Johanna felt. When Johanna paused and took a sip from her travel coffee mug, she faced Payton again. "I still don't understand why Mom and Dad are selling the house."

Even during Dad's health crisis, Johanna couldn't let go of this issue.

"They probably lived here longer than they've needed to."

Johanna stilled. "Why do you say that?"

"Don't you remember? They'd planned on moving before Pepper died. They'd found that house with the great view of Pikes Peak."

"I'd forgotten about that."

"I remember it had a deck. The same number of bedrooms, but Dad said one would be his office. Think about it, Jo. You and Jillian were both away at college and Pepper and I were already juniors in high school.

Mom liked that it was closer to Dad's work, so he'd have less of a commute." Payton was surprised how easily she could talk about the memory. "But then Pepper died and well, life stopped . . . because everything changed."

"I can understand how it seemed like that for you. It was different for me. I went back to college . . ."

"Life got back to normal."

"Yes. In a lot of ways, I didn't have to think about what had happened." Johanna offered Payton a weak smile. "That sounds horrible."

"No. No, there were days I wished I could stop thinking about her. *That* sounds horrible, doesn't it?"

Johanna gripped her coffee mug, her gaze never wavering. "You and Pepper were always so close—in a way I never understood."

"You and Jillian have always been close—"

"Yes." Johanna nodded. "But the twin thing . . . it's different."

Payton couldn't disagree with Johanna because what she said was true.

They were treading so cautiously on new ground. Talking about Pepper without either of them getting upset. There was no tension in Payton's neck or shoulders. No harsh words choking her, waiting to be hurled at her sister.

Moments like this, as brief as they were, gave Payton hope for the future with Johanna. Their relationship would never be perfect. They'd always clash. But she'd work harder for moments like this.

Of course, she was moving to England in six months. How would that affect her relationship with Johanna? With Jillian?

"I've always loved this house." Johanna's comment was an abrupt change of subject.

"Really?"

"I like the central location. And the street is quiet with some mature trees. The kitchen is a good size—but honestly, I'd knock out that wall and open it up to the dining room."

"I wonder if Mom ever thought about doing that." Payton tried to imagine the kitchen and dining room as an open concept. "Did you ever want your own bedroom?"

"Every girl wants her own bedroom, Payton." They shared a laugh. "But the rooms are decent size. Of course, the closets could be bigger."

"True, true."

"The family room is probably my favorite place." Johanna's voice was quiet, as if she were recalling the countless Sundays spent there, watching football games with Dad. Playing board games. All the Christmas mornings they'd run downstairs to see the presents piled around the tree, their once-empty stockings decorating the fireplace mantel now full. "I'd update the fireplace—"

"What? I love the fireplace."

"I do, too, but I'd do a different face on it—or maybe paint the brick and replace the mantel."

They'd backed away from a personal conversation,

but they were still talking. No impatience in Johanna's voice. No irritation. Jillian would never believe this minor morning miracle.

Maybe, just maybe, Johanna liked her.

Not that Payton was going to ask her.

"Do you think it would be okay for me to call Mom again?"

And now Johanna was asking her opinion?

"She'll call when she has something to tell us."

"You're right. I know you're right." Johanna crossed her arms, rubbing her hands up and down her forearms against the soft material of her white sweater. "I just wish I could be there when the doctor talks with them."

"You know even better than I do how doctors have their own schedule. There's no telling when a doctor will show up."

"I know."

"Have you talked to Jillian today?" Payton leaned down, resting her arms on the island, her chin in her hands.

"I called her on my way down."

"And?"

"She's doing okay. Didn't sleep too well, but I don't think any of us did."

"Dad's going to be okay." She'd alternated between praying and telling herself this all night.

Johanna was silent for a moment. And then . . . "He has to be. I can't imagine Mom without . . ."

Johanna's voice cracked. She was saying aloud what

Payton couldn't. What Jillian was thinking. Mom without Dad . . . or Dad without Mom . . . the thought made no sense.

Payton wanted to hug her big sister. But there was no need to be hasty, to push the closeness they'd shared.

"I-I think I'm going to run the vacuum." Johanna straightened her shoulders, her voice devoid of emotion.

"Vacuum?"

"Just in the front room. And the hallway. It can't hurt."

She wasn't going to argue with Johanna. Let her vacuum the entire house—it would keep her busy while she waited for Mom to call.

"I'm going to take Mom the things she asked for and then I need to run some errands. We have open gym this weekend for club and I want to have Christmas gifts for the girls."

"Every girl?"

"Something small. Even ChapStick and some chocolate works." Payton risked a quick half hug. "I'll grab what Mom wanted and leave you to your vacuuming."

"Let me know if you hear from Mom."

"You do the same, Jo."

"It's times like now I wish we could do a conference call."

"Well, I know you can figure that out—" Payton

paused. "Tell you what, if Mom calls you first, tell her that you'll call me and Jillian. Take the stress off her."

"I'll do that."

"Why don't you just text her and tell her. Have her call you and tell her you'll let Jillian and me know what's going on."

"Great idea."

Of course it was—Johanna was in charge.

But that was fine. Johanna hadn't demanded anything. Payton had suggested the plan because it made sense. Helped Mom, who didn't need to be making multiple phone calls. This was a concession . . . but an easy one. A willing one on Payton's part.

A smile reached Johanna's blue eyes for the first time that morning.

Payton had started the day off making Johanna smile. Imagine that.

It was going to be a good day.

THE DOOR TO DON'S HOSPITAL ROOM CLOSED AS THE cardiac electrophysiologist left. Don and I were alone again. Did the air in the room seem thin only to me? What if I had more questions before Don's surgery tomorrow? Not that I could think of any right now—I was still trying to process the information we did have.

"Well, that conversation was brief and to the point." Acid burned in the back of my throat, all the way down to my stomach. I'd had too many cups of coffee since coming to the hospital on Sunday, not that they'd helped. The caffeine merely masked my exhaustion.

"What did you expect, Heather?" Don offered me an understanding smile, as if I was the patient, not him. "A cozy chat about our families? We're not the woman's only patients."

"No, of course not. I understand she's busy. But it all seemed so . . . quick."

"She answered all our questions. The procedure sounds pretty straightforward."

I lowered myself to the chair beside Don's bed, easing the ache in my lower back. When he reached for my hand, I clasped his, palm to palm.

"I hope you cleared your calendar for the rest of December." I infused a light note into my words.

"I don't think I have much say in the matter."

"No. We'll do what the cardiologist says, which means surgery for you sometime tomorrow."

"I don't know how I feel about a pacemaker—" Don rested his other hand on his chest.

"What do you mean? It'll keep you alive."

"It's just odd to think I'll have a piece of machinery attached to my heart."

"I'm thankful for that piece of machinery." I leaned closer, squeezing his hand. "Once I tell Johanna, she's going to research it."

"See? We don't need to worry about talking to the cardiologist. Tell Johanna to find out if I can go through TSA when we travel."

"Duly noted, but not any time soon." I smoothed

the blanket covering his legs. "Are you worried about surgery?"

"No. I'm choosing to trust the cardiologist. She's the expert, so she knows what she's doing. And Johanna will research her too."

"True." My phone pinged. "Tracey is texting, asking if this is a good time to talk."

"Go ahead and call her." Don closed his eyes. "I'll rest for a few moments."

Our agent answered after the first ring. "Tracey, I'm so sorry I've been unavailable—"

"Nonsense, Heather. How is Don doing?"

"He has an irregular heartbeat. The cardiologist is doing surgery tomorrow to implant a pacemaker."

"Goodness, that sounds serious."

"Yes—all of this is so unexpected. But I'm thankful the issue is being taken care of."

"I know you're probably not even thinking about the house sale right now—"

"That's true. I haven't left the hospital since yesterday."

"Completely understandable. I haven't spoken to the buyers again yet because I wanted to talk with you first. Are you still wanting to sell the house with everything else going on?"

"I believe so—we haven't talked about *not* selling the house." I tapped Don's arm and he gave me an okay sign. "Yes—there's no need to change anything. If we could postpone the necessary paperwork until after Don's surgery, that might help . . ."

"I don't think that would be a problem at all. I'll call them now and get back with you."

After disconnecting the call, I set my phone on the little side table next to the hospital bed and closed my eyes while I rubbed my temples.

"You okay?"

"There's just a lot going on." I inhaled and exhaled. Opened my eyes. "I need to catch my breath."

"Have you even had breakfast yet?"

"I went to the cafeteria before you woke up and got some fresh fruit and scrambled eggs, but I didn't have much of an appetite. Coffee is flowing freely through my veins right now—too much coffee, to be honest."

"Heather, I've always said our daughters learned their coffee-drinking habits from you."

I leaned over the guard rail and kissed his cheek, ignoring the bit of scruff on his face. "And I've never disagreed with you about that. But I need to stick with water for the rest of the day."

"Why don't you sleep at home tonight? Get some rest before my surgery tomorrow?"

"We've already discussed this. I would just lie awake all night in our bed, worrying about you here in the hospital. So long as they don't kick me out of here, I'm staying." I offered Don my best "I'm fine" smile. "I asked Payton to bring me a change of clothes, but now I'm thinking I may run home later and take a shower, if that's okay. One of the girls will have to come get me because I don't have a car here."

"You know any of the girls will do that—all you have to do is ask."

"And that's the dilemma—who do I ask without hurting the other two?"

"You can always draw a name from a hat."

"No hats here."

"You don't have to decide right this minute. Why don't you wait until Payton gets here and discuss it with her?"

"You're right—you usually are."

"Now you're just flattering me." My husband's voice turned serious. "We'll be okay, Heather."

"*You'll* be okay, Don." I fought to keep my voice light as I gripped his hand again. "We have so much good ahead of us. We've just bought a house. We're selling a house. Christmas is less than three weeks away."

"I'm not going anywhere, Heather."

It was as if, here in this hospital room, we were making solemn vows to one another. Promises didn't happen just in churches during wedding ceremonies. They continued again and again throughout a marriage, as needed.

It was turning into a snowy Monday. The light snowfall predicted for the morning commute was lingering, not a bit of sunlight in the skies overhead. Jillian was thankful the roads were still mostly wet and that she wouldn't be one of the commuters dealing with icy conditions if the storm lasted through the evening.

She left her car on, heater running, as she sat parked outside Geoff's workplace. A nap sounded good right about now. Between her normal struggle with exhaustion, the stress of her dad's hospitalization, and the snow, she could have opted out of bringing Geoff lunch today. But she wanted this—a chance to connect, even if just for a few minutes. She would have a nap later, although she'd dubbed her naps *siestas* because that sounded a bit nicer.

Jillian was coming up on three years post her mastectomy and chemotherapy, and yet naps were still an everyday occurrence. She no longer wrestled with guilt about it—most days. The fact that she worked from home doing very part-time accounting for a local start-up company gave her a sense of satisfaction.

"Thanks for bringing me lunch." Geoff slipped into the passenger seat of her Subaru, shutting the door quickly to keep out the cold winter air. He leaned over and gave her a kiss as she handed him the insulated bag containing a ham sandwich with cheddar cheese, sour cream and onion potato chips, homemade snickerdoodles, and a red pear.

"I know I usually do this later in the week, but yesterday was so unsettling. I'm still trying to process what happened with Dad . . ."

And the conversation they'd started Friday night and never finished hadn't been a good one.

Twisting, Geoff set the bagged lunch at his feet and leaned against the door. "I know you're worried about Dad. I am too."

"Johanna called just a little while ago to say Dad's going to have surgery sometime tomorrow to have a pacemaker put in."

"A pacemaker." Geoff's hazel eyes widened behind his glasses. "That never occurred to me."

"I don't think any of us thought of something like that. Dad's heartbeat is irregular—sometimes too fast, sometimes too slow." Jillian paused, staring at the light snow blanketing the front windshield despite the heater. "But the pacemaker will fix the problem. That's the important thing."

Geoff leaned close, his half-embrace a bit awkward in the car. "He'll be fine."

"I have to believe that. I do believe that. I haven't stopped praying since Zach called yesterday."

"I know." Geoff settled back against the passenger seat. "Do you know what time the surgery is scheduled for?"

"Not yet. Again, Mom's going to call Johanna and then she'll update me and Payton—it's easier for her to let Johanna update us."

Geoff reached over and took her hand. "I'll talk to my boss. Take the day off."

"Thank you." Jillian tucked a lock of her hair behind her ear. "Brian's wife checked in again, which I thought was so kind. I'm sorry we can't go see them this Christmas."

"It's not the right time, not with your parents moving and now Dad's surgery."

"I know, but you were excited about seeing your brother."

"We'll try to make a trip in the spring."

Geoff was being Geoff. Understanding. Supportive. And their relationship was stronger than it had been two years ago. They'd concentrated on their marriage. On fun things like discovering favorite hikes and experimenting with new recipes and even purchasing a tandem bike.

They'd focused on hope.

Geoff reached for the door handle, as if he was ready to head back to work.

Was work so busy today? Or was he avoiding any possibility of their conversation veering into difficult topics? Jillian should say goodbye, let him get back to his office.

But was it so wrong to want a few more minutes with her husband?

Was it so wrong, after all these months, to want to talk?

She might as well say something—anything—to try and ease the lingering tension between them. "I know our conversation Friday night wasn't great."

"You want to talk about this *now*?" Geoff removed his glasses and pressed his fingers against his closed eyelids.

"I don't want to talk about it, no." The car seemed

warmer, as if she'd ratcheted up the heat. "I just wanted to say I'm sorry—"

His gaze collided with hers. "Sorry you brought up the topic of children again?"

She was not apologizing for that.

"No. We agreed to table the topic for two years. We've passed that deadline by a few months. One of us had to say something."

"During the holidays?"

"I'm sorry if my timing was off." Jillian risked resting her hand on Geoff's forearm. "Is there a time you'd like to talk about it? January, maybe?"

"Is this the time to push the issue, Jill?"

She pulled her hand away. "I'm not pushing the issue. We tabled the topic of children, but we never addressed how to start talking about it again."

"Or *if* we wanted to talk about it again."

Jillian's throat tightened. "Wh-what do you mean?"

"What if how we . . . how *I* feel hasn't changed?" His question was void of emotion.

Geoff's words were like heavy boots stomping on a fragile seedling. She'd hoped he'd be more open to the idea of starting a family. Of pursuing infertility treatments or even adoption, which could happen sooner.

With each passing day, she'd fallen more in love with her husband. Accepted who she was—a cancer survivor. But she'd never stopped hoping their family would one day be more than the two of them—and Winston.

With all the prayers she'd prayed with Payton

during the last two years, why hadn't Geoff's heart changed?

"Even if how . . . how we feel hasn't changed, we have to talk about it." Jillian raised her hand to stop Geoff from interrupting her. "Not here and now, obviously. You have to go back to work. And what's going on with Dad is more important. So maybe . . . maybe we agree to talk in January."

Geoff nodded, retrieving his lunch. "January it is."

"And I don't mean New Year's Day. We'll look at the calendar and pick a day and time."

"Fair enough. I'm going to head inside and eat my lunch." He raised the lunch bag. "Thanks for this."

"You're welcome. I love you." She leaned forward, grateful when Geoff met her halfway for a kiss. "I do love you, Geoff. We'll figure this out."

"I love you too." Geoff stole another swift kiss. "Let me know when you hear something about Dad. And I'll get tomorrow off."

"Thank you."

Saying "I love you" anchored them back to their common ground. No matter what, they loved one another. That was always, always true. Her best friend, Harper, had taught her that.

I haven't forgotten, Harper. I won't forget.

Geoff stopped to talk to a coworker on his way back to his office building. Threw his head back as they both laughed.

How she loved Geoff's laugh. His jokes.

They'd had so much fun the last two years, but life

wasn't all fun and games and tandem bike rides. Some-times the hard stuff needed to be faced.

Just as she started her car, her phone rang.

Johanna.

Jillian left the car in park. "Did you hear from Mom?"

"Yes. I just got off the phone with her."

"Do they have a time for Dad's surgery?"

"He's scheduled for seven o'clock tomorrow morning."

Jillian gripped the steering wheel, scanning the parking lot, but Geoff was already inside the building. "That's what we were waiting to find out. Geoff's plan-ning to take the day off."

"Beckett will too. I'm going to see if I can get someone to stay with Ellison. I was thinking Axton's wife might help."

"It's nice how you've developed a friendship with them."

"Who would have thought, right? Uncle Axton and Aunt Dot." Johanna laughed. "Oh, one more thing."

"Is there a problem?"

"No. Mom wanted me to ask you to call her when you had a chance. She needs to ask you something."

"Okay. I can do that. Do you know what she wants?"

"No. Maybe she just wants to check in with you, see how you're doing."

"That sounds like Mom."

"I'll talk with you later. I'm going to call Aunt Dot."

"Wait—how are you doing?"

"Me?" There was silence on the line for just a moment. "I'm fine so long as I keep busy. And I keep telling myself things could have been so much worse. By tomorrow afternoon Dad will have his new pacemaker and be on the other side of all this."

"Right. We just need to get through tomorrow."

This was some sort of drink-this-it's-good-for-you yucky medicine. They had a diagnosis. They had a treatment. Yes, it could be worse. But the thought of Dad needing surgery . . . a pacemaker . . . it all seemed so wrong.

Despite the hot air flowing through the vents in the dash, Jillian was chilled. She could go get Geoff. Interrupt his lunch and ask for a hug—a nice, long one.

No. No, she wouldn't do that. She'd talk to him once he got home.

"Right. Tomorrow. Although I won't take a full, deep breath until Dad's home." Jillian released the steering wheel and flexed her fingers. "What did Mom say about visitors tonight?"

"Two at a time, and of course, Ellison is too young to see Dad. We learned that the last time we brought her with us."

"So it sounds like we do shifts."

"Yes. Beckett is going to stay with Ellison this evening so I can see Dad. We'll all figure out how we want to coordinate things."

"Sounds good. We can text each other and figure

out who sees Dad when. Geoff is usually home by 6:30. No big projects right now."

"Okay. I'll send a group text to Payton and you and we'll get tonight set."

Jillian ended the call, thankful there'd been no emotional tug of war with Johanna. Yes, she was manning communication central, but she wasn't declaring herself king of the hill—or rather, queen of the hill.

Jillian pressed her fist against the tightness centered under her sternum. She didn't want to get into a tug of war with Geoff either. She wanted them to talk to each other. To listen to each other.

And to hope, always hope, there was a possibility he'd hear her, despite his heartaches of the past.

JILLIAN'S PARENTS' HOME ALWAYS LOOKED NEAT. Organized. Long ago, Mom had adopted the "a place for everything, and everything in its place" method of keeping the house clean. And yet, it was still comfortable. Since deciding to sell the house, Mom and Dad had put an extra layer of shine on everything. A faint scent of citrus lingered in the air, probably because Mom had polished all the wood furniture, the stair railings—most likely even the baseboards. Windows and mirrors? Spotless. Fresh flowers, all with red and green and white holiday colors, were placed in several of the rooms, and Jillian was certain those weren't from Dad.

Her phone pinged a text from Geoff.

Geoff: *How's your afternoon going?*
Jillian: *Good. Mom asked me to bring her home so she could shower and get more clean clothes before spending the night at the hospital again. I'm there now.*
Geoff: *What's the latest?*
Jillian: *The surgery for the pacemaker is still scheduled for 7 tomorrow morning.*
Geoff: *How are you feeling?*
Jillian: *Thankful to have a diagnosis and treatment. Mom feels confident, so that's good.*
Geoff: *I'll call when I get off work and see where you are.*
Jillian: *Okay. Love you.*
Geoff: *Love you too.*

Her earlier phone call to update him about Dad's surgery had erased the tension between them. The topic of their future, of children, tabled once again by this more pressing emergency.

Setting her phone back on the kitchen counter next to her purse, Jillian picked up her Styrofoam cup of coffee and wandered through the quiet house, thankful Mom had requested a quick drive-through for a decaf coffee on the way to the house. She'd missed her siesta, but Jillian was more than happy to help her mom today.

The small tree with white lights in front of the living room window along with the small door wreath was the only nod to Christmas in the house. Mom always centered a large, live tree in the front window and loved to decorate the stair rails and the fireplace mantel with garland, while displaying her Christmas village on the dining room buffet. For years, Dad added a new piece every Christmas until Mom declared her collection complete and vetoed Dad's suggestion to start a neighboring village.

Moments later, Mom found her snuggled in Dad's recliner in the downstairs family room, wrapped in one of the older blue-and-orange fleece Broncos blankets Mom kept piled in a basket.

"You okay, Jillian?" Mom's voice was soft with concern.

"Yes. This seemed like a good place to wait for you." She hesitated. "I was . . . praying for Dad."

"Oh." Mom smiled. "That's nice."

Nice.

"I'm praying for the surgeon and all the people who will be taking care of Dad tomorrow during the surgery . . . and I'm praying for you and Dad to have peace through all this."

"Thank you, Jillian." Mom settled on the couch, offering her a smile bracketed with lines that gave away her weariness. Her worry. "I appreciate that. I know Dad would too."

"How are you doing, Mom?" Jillian pulled the soft blanket tighter.

"Good. I mean, I'll be glad to get home and sleep in

my own bed again"—Mom shrugged, as if her confession was no surprise—"but I'm thankful I can be with your dad. And it's only two more nights."

"Did you get everything you need?"

"I think so. I just tossed all my dirty clothes in the laundry hamper and repacked the bag. Your dad told me to bring him a book to read, but I don't think he'll be doing a lot of reading after his surgery."

"Well, take it anyway." Jillian stood and folded the blanket back up, leaving it on the back of Dad's chair as they headed upstairs. "I noticed a couple of agents' cards on the kitchen counter."

"I did too—but when I spoke to Tracey earlier today she said the buyer is still interested in this house, despite the delay."

"That's good. I'll get our drinks and my purse. Do you want me to leave any lights on?"

"Everything is on a timer, which is more convenient than I realized it would be."

A few moments later, they were settled in Jillian's car and headed back to the hospital.

"How are you doing, Jilly?"

"Me?" Mom's repeated question surprised her. "I'm fine. Really."

"Are you worried about your dad? You seem . . . I don't know, sad today. Or maybe my mother's intuition is off."

For just a moment, Jillian was tempted to deny what Mom had discerned. She had enough to deal with already with Dad's pacemaker surgery.

But sometimes a daughter needed her mother—even if she was grown up, married, and it wasn't the best time.

"Geoff and I . . ." How could she explain it? "We had a tough conversation this morning. Not a fight, really . . . just a disagreement, I guess."

"May I ask what it was about? I don't want to pry—"

"Children."

"Oh."

Jillian blinked hard and fast against the rush of tears. She was driving a car and the roads were a bit slick, thanks to the earlier snowfall. This was not the time to cry.

"I told you when we were having lunch on Sunday —that seems so long ago—how we haven't talked about children for two years. When I tried to bring it up again, it didn't go well.

"Geoff doesn't want children?"

"It's complicated, but no, he doesn't—that's how he felt two years ago. I was hoping he'd changed his mind. That maybe he would consider adopting if I can't get pregnant."

"Are you so sure you can't get pregnant?"

And now she had to face once again the most critical way cancer had changed her life. She'd adapted to the mastectomy. To her forgetfulness. Her tiredness. But this . . .

"Well, I can't even try to get pregnant while I'm on some of my medications. And infertility is one of the consequences I might face. Adoption might be the only way we can have a family."

"Oh, Jillian, if you told me this and I forgot—"

"It's okay, Mom. A lot has happened since I was first diagnosed."

"So you brought the topic of wanting to start a family up, and Geoff..."

"Geoff was upset. He didn't yell or anything—that's not Geoff at all. But he just shut me out. We had a very quiet weekend. I'm not sure what to do."

"If you're asking me what I think you should do..." Mom's voice trailed off.

"Yes. Yes, I am."

"Stalemate is not an option. It works for a chess game, but not for real life. I don't think this is about compromise. You and Geoff have to find a yes or no answer that both of you agree on."

"But how do we do that?"

"It's going to take hard conversations, uncomfortable conversations, but they have to happen." Mom took a deep breath. "I wish I'd talked more about Pepper's death sooner. I wish your dad and I had talked more with each other. It was one of the most difficult times in our marriage. We didn't talk to one another about how we were feeling for months. We both grieved so differently—and it was the one time we let something drive us apart."

Jillian had never heard Mom talk about how Pepper's death had affected her and Dad.

"What helped you start talking?"

"I found your dad sitting in Pepper and Payton's bedroom one night—this was when we'd sent Payton to the medical facility for some psychological help—and he was crying. He hadn't cried since the night Pepper died. Or at least, I didn't know he'd cried."

"Oh, Mom . . ."

"We sat in the room for several hours, crying together . . . I listened to how he felt and over the next few months we found our way back to each other. It was the start of a conversation we should have had so much sooner."

Jillian stared straight ahead as she waited for a stoplight to change to green. "I tried to start the conversation with Geoff and it didn't go well."

"Then you try again." Mom's tone was firm. "It's not an optional conversation."

"You're right. I know you're right."

"I know God is important to you, Jill. You're praying for your dad. I assume you're praying about this too."

"Yes."

"Well then, I would imagine that helps." Mom patted her hand where it rested on the steering wheel.

"Thanks, Mom."

"You're welcome. Thanks for talking to me."

Yes, prayer did help. Today was about supporting Mom, but God had used her in such an unexpected way to renew Jillian's hope.

7

I'd expected things to be a little quieter our first day back home from the hospital after Don's surgery, and in some ways, they were. No monitors beeping. No nurses or medical technicians going in and out of Don's room. But I'd underestimated both our neighbors and our daughters.

The various neighbors hadn't asked to see Don when they dropped off an assortment of meals, but there was no stopping Johanna or Jillian or Payton when they showed up at the door to check on their dad. I couldn't blame them—I only resisted peeking in on him when he was napping.

Johanna, Beckett, and sweet Ellison visited with Don now, promising to keep their time brief. Don's laugh blended with Ellison's smile-inducing giggle as I left our bedroom in search of my abandoned cup of coffee. Somewhere in the house there were at least three cups of coffee that I'd set down and lost track of throughout the afternoon.

I'd start my search in the kitchen.

A crockpot of broccoli cheddar soup scented the kitchen, the aroma mingling with the bran muffins Ellison declared she'd made herself. Meals of lasagna, chili, and vegetable soup, along with homemade bread, were tucked into my fridge and I was thankful I didn't have to worry about cooking for the next several days.

Relief and fatigue warred within my body, and my muscles ached for a long, hot shower and the chance to crawl into bed next to Don. But I knew I wouldn't sleep right away. Just like in the hospital, I'd lie awake, watching him breathe, willing him to be okay. To stay with me. As if my thoughts controlled his heartbeat, not the newly installed pacemaker.

No coffee mug here. Just a scattered pile of mail on the island that would have to wait until the morning, unless insomnia brought me back downstairs in the middle of the night and prompted me to deal with things then.

"Mom?" Payton's voice sounded from the front hallway. "Where are you?"

"I'm here." I moved through the dining room, still searching for my lost coffee.

Payton and Zach joined me, her cheerful red sweater a nod to the season. "We came to check on Dad. We won't stay long."

"That's exactly what both of your sisters said when they came to see him."

"Are they here now?"

"Johanna is—with Beckett and Ellison. Jillian and Geoff have already headed home."

"How's Dad doing?" Payton leaned in for a hug, then Zach.

"He's tired, but I know he'll sleep better now that he's home."

"I imagine you both will."

"Yes." No need to confess my plan to watch her dad sleep.

"Is it okay if we just peek in on him, say hello? Maybe hug him really, really gently?" Payton's eyes welled up with tears.

"Of course. He'll love seeing both of you." I looped my arms through theirs and we headed for the stairs. "Well, there's no way we'll all three fit, so you two go ahead."

"Should we wait for Johanna and Beckett?"

"Your arrival will remind them that they promised not to stay long. Knowing Johanna, she's providing information about his pacemaker."

We shared a conspiratorial laugh. "Johanna and her research. She may just have skipped Google and called the company."

But when we walked into the room, Johanna sat at the head of the bed, holding her dad's hand, while Beckett kept Ellison corralled by holding her on his back. Our granddaughter's handmade get-well card, all rainbow scribbles with a lopsided Rudolph, sat on the bedside table nearest Don.

"Payton and Zach!" Don's eyes warmed with a smile despite the lines etched around the corners, just as they had when Jillian and Geoff and then Johanna, Beckett, and Ellison had arrived. "Well, now the day is complete, isn't it, Heather?"

"Hi, Dad." Payton's greeting was barely above a whisper. "We just wanted to drop by for a few minutes—"

"That's what we've all said." Johanna squeezed her dad's hand and stood. "We'll head home now so you can talk with Payton and Zach."

"Tell Grandpa goodbye, Ellison."

"Come give me a kiss." Don held out his arms and cradled Ellison close for a few seconds, careful to keep her away from his pacemaker site. "That's the best medicine."

"Payton, you and Zach visit with your dad. I'll walk Johanna and Beckett to the door." I reached for my granddaughter. "Let me carry my namesake."

"Gloating again?" Don raised an eyebrow.

"Never. Just enjoying the fact that she has my maiden name."

Ellison wrapped her arms around my neck as I followed Johanna and Beckett back downstairs. But just as we got to the front door, my cell phone rang from the kitchen.

"Mom, let me take her and you go get that." Johanna took Ellison from me.

"It's okay, whoever it is can leave a message."

"But it could be the doctor checking on Dad—"

"Oh—you're right." I waved a quick goodbye and double-timed it to the kitchen, catching the phone on the third ring, just before it turned over to voicemail. "Hello? This is Heather."

"Heather? This is Tracey. I wasn't sure I'd catch you. Are you home from the hospital?"

"Yes, we came home earlier this afternoon."

"So that's it, then? The pacemaker will correct the issue?"

"Yes. Don's resting upstairs." Retrieving a mug from the cupboard, I placed a pod in the Keurig, and set the mug on the base. "Did you call about the closing? If you need to bring paperwork by—"

"Heather, I hate to tell you this when Don's just had surgery, but the sale fell through."

I gripped the edge of the counter so that my knuckles whitened. "Fell through? Why? I thought you said it was a good offer . . ."

"It was a good offer. But when I told the buyers things were delayed, even explaining there was a medical emergency, they decided to look at some more houses, just to see if there was anything else they liked better than your house."

"I guess they found something."

"Their agent called me about half an hour ago. I'm so sorry."

Coffee streamed into my mug, but the aroma soured my stomach. "It's not your fault."

"Are you interested in doing another open house this weekend?"

"This weekend? I don't think so. Don just got home and he needs to rest. And to be honest, so do I. Maybe we need to hold off on showing the house for the rest of the month."

"I know you've been through a lot. Why don't you talk with Don and I'll call again on Monday? I'll let you know if anyone is interested in seeing the house."

"Fine. Thanks for calling."

"Again, I'm sorry."

We hung up after brief goodbyes. The bitter odor of coffee lingered in the air. I took the mug and dumped it in the sink, turning on the faucet and rinsing the brown liquid so it flowed down the drain.

So much for the full-price cash offer on the house.

Were we wrong about selling the house? Should we just take it off the market?

It was too late to be rethinking our decision. We were closing on our new house in February. We *had* to sell this house.

"You okay, Mom?" Payton's question startled me.

I whirled around to face her. "I thought you were still with your dad."

"We promised not to stay long, remember?" Payton and Zach both stood just inside the kitchen. "You look upset."

"Tracey just called. The offer on the house fell through. The buyers got impatient and found another house they liked better."

"Oh, Mom. I'm so sorry." When Payton wrapped me in a hug, I allowed myself to rest my head on her shoulder for a moment. "What now?"

"I told Tracey that I need at least the weekend to think about this. We can't back out of our contract, so we need to sell this house."

"There's still time to find a buyer—and who knows? You might get another cash offer."

"Yes." I stepped back and straightened my shoulders. Time to be in control again. "But it was so nice that we'd found our buyer the first weekend."

"When are you going to tell Dad?"

"Not tonight. He needs a good night's sleep."

"And so do you."

"I'll get one, now that we're home and your dad's surgery is behind us."

Zach took hold of one of my hands. "We're praying for both of you."

"Oh, don't worry about me." I infused my words with as much confidence as I could. "Your dad's the one who had the surgery."

Payton peered into my eyes. "You look just as exhausted as Dad."

I had to laugh, knowing it was true. "Thanks for that."

"Payton means well." Zach nudged his wife. "Dad may be asleep by the time you get up there."

"Then I'd better go and help him get ready for bed."

"We'll let ourselves out." Payton hugged me again. "You go take care of Dad."

"Thank you." I accepted a hug from Zach. "It's good to see you both."

Payton paused just inside the kitchen doorway. "Is it okay if we mention the house issue to Johanna and Jill?"

"That's fine, but tell them it's not a topic of conversation with your dad."

"Absolutely."

After they left, I turned out lights and headed back upstairs, leaving the small Christmas tree with its white lights on so that it cast a soft glow in the living room. The smallest bit of Christmas cheer that I needed.

Even with the lights on, Don had fallen asleep in our bed, the blankets pulled up around his shoulders. I'd let him sleep, reminding him to brush his teeth if he woke up in the middle of the night, which was unlikely.

Until then, I turned off the bedroom lights and settled myself in the high-backed upholstered chair near our bedroom window. Turned on the small light on the table nearby and picked up the book I'd tried to read while I was at the hospital. I doubted I'd make much progress with the cozy mystery tonight, but I could try.

Instead of reading, I found myself listening to— and counting—Don's soft breaths that filled the room.

Inhale. Exhale.

Thank you.

Inhale. Exhale.

Thank you.

But who was I thanking?

Payton and Jillian would thank God, but I didn't have their faith. Had never wanted a relationship with God, some sort of heavenly father who might be just like my father . . .

Unreliable.

Unknowable.

Self-centered.

My father was probably dead by now . . . I didn't know. I'd lost track of both him and my mom years ago . . . or rather, they'd disappeared. Phone disconnected. A Christmas card returned, marked *Addressee Unknown*.

"They're probably off on some new adventure." Don stood next to me in the kitchen, knowing not to touch me when I was upset and trying to act like I wasn't.

"Right. The next big thing." I tossed the envelope in the trash. "Or dead."

"Heather!"

"I don't know . . ." My voice cracked. Such a waste of emotion. "I don't know why I even bothered to send them a card when last year's was returned."

Don wrapped me in his arms. "We've got each other. We've got the girls."

"Yes—and that's all that matters."

I shook the memory—the melancholy—away. That was years ago. Whenever our daughters asked about my parents, we said they'd died. It was easier that way.

And they'd never made a surprise, unannounced appearance in our lives—only to disappear again after creating all sorts of questions I didn't want to answer.

That was the best gift my parents ever gave me.

$\mathcal{S}$unday looked like some sort of bizarre early arrival of Christmas morning gone wrong with all the brown packing boxes scattered around the family room. The fresh pine bough with berries and pinecones woven throughout it gracing the mantel scented the air. Payton had put on *Frosty the Snowman* for Ellison, who clapped her hands as Frosty, wearing his magic hat, marched through the town with the children.

"Did your Realtor okay this?" Payton motioned toward the mantel.

"I didn't bother to get her okay." Mom handed Payton a cup of hot chocolate topped with marshmallows. "These are the vegan brand you told me about."

"Thanks, Mom, but you didn't have to go to the bother of buying special marshmallows for me."

"Everybody gets marshmallows at Christmastime." Mom bussed her cheek with a light kiss.

"How are you and dad doing?"

"Every time I see the For Sale sign still up in the yard without Under Contract on it, I'm so disappointed." She paused and then voiced the thought that had shadowed her for days. "Maybe we were too hasty buying that house in Briargate."

"But you and Dad love it. I'm excited to see it."

"There just hasn't been any time." Mom motioned to Dad sitting in his recliner and scratching Winston's fluffy white ears as he snuggled in his lap. "I'm glad Jillian and Geoff brought Winston."

"Dad loves that dog. Maybe you and Dad—"

"Don't say it, Payton. This isn't the time to even think about getting a puppy."

"Maybe when you get settled into your new house? What do you think, Dad? Start the New Year with a new house and a new puppy?"

"I've tried to talk your mom into getting a dog for years." Dad grinned as he ruffled Winston's ears.

"That's all I need to worry about—housebreaking a puppy in our new home."

Payton sipped her hot chocolate, licking away the marshmallow clinging to her top lip. "At least Winston's keeping Dad occupied while the rest of us sort through these boxes."

"Thanks to Johanna's prep, we'll get a lot accomplished today."

"Honestly, Mom, we should have come over and claimed—or thrown away—this stuff years ago."

"I didn't mind it being in the attic. What's your

parents' house for if not to store all the stuff you've forgotten about?"

Payton had to laugh. "I've discovered textbooks from when Pepper and I were in high school—some double copies, of course. No one needs high school algebra or English comp notebooks."

"You're right about that."

"I'm keeping our yearbooks—unless you want Pepper's."

Mom paused. "I think I would like Pepper's yearbooks, if you don't mind. I don't think I ever looked through them. It would be . . . nice to see her again after all these years."

Payton retrieved the trio of books from the box she'd been filling with items she planned to take home. "Make sure to read the messages friends wrote inside the ones from our freshman and sophomore years. You'll like those. I didn't have anyone write anything in them when we were juniors—obviously. But there's a special dedication in memory of Pepper in the yearbook for our senior year. Did you and Dad ever see it?"

"I remember you saying something about the dedication back then—your dad and I read it when you brought it home. But I think it would be nice to read it again." Mom cradled the books in her arms. "So much has changed."

"Yes. For the better."

And sometime today, she and Zach needed to tell their family how things were going to be changing again.

It wasn't until they were halfway through lunch that Payton found an opening in the activity and conversation. Beckett had laid Ellison down for a nap in one of the bedrooms upstairs. Winston dozed by the fireplace in the family room. Some of the boxes had been lugged out to different cars or taken to the garage for trash pickup.

The family sat around the dining room table, savoring leftovers from various meals brought by the neighbors.

"Quite a smorgasbord here, isn't it?" Dad had settled on a bowl of vegetable soup and homemade bread.

"I've appreciated not having to cook." Mom grinned as she sliced into her lasagna.

"What are the neighbors bringing next week?" Geoff's plate overflowed with a sampling of everything.

"Geoff!" Jillian laughed, nudging his shoulder.

"I'm not sure, but thank you for bringing the taco pie."

"And Jill made two of those, so there's one at home for us."

Payton allowed the verbal back and forth to continue, trying to find a way to interrupt, almost like trying to merge into traffic.

"Zach and I wanted to discuss something—"

"Sorry—there are only two taco pies." Geoff grinned, nudging his glasses back up on his nose.

"Duly noted. No taco pies for us." Payton reached

for Zach's hand under the table. "Um, it's not about food. Not even close."

"Is everything okay?" Johanna set her glass down.

"Is this a surprise?" Jillian took a more positive approach.

"Yes, I'm okay. Yes, yes, you could say this is a surprise—"

"Are you pregnant?" Mom's voice pitched high.

Payton froze. That was Mom's guess? Had she even mentioned anything about wanting to start a family?

"No! I'm not pregnant." Payton made eye contact with Jillian, who'd gone white.

"We're moving." Zach's voice broke the tension surrounding the table.

"Zach!" Payton turned to face him.

"What?" Zach shrugged. "I figured it would stop all the guessing."

"You're . . . *moving?*" Now Johanna's face paled. "Where?"

There was no dodging her sister's direct question.

"England."

"*England?* You're moving *overseas?*" Johanna's words were an accusation.

And now . . . now Zach had gone silent on her.

"Zach has a wonderful opportunity to work with a master craftsman—he'll learn so much about cabinetry and building furniture. He's been talking to Alfred—that's the man's name—for months now. And he . . . and after praying about it, he . . . *we* knew he couldn't pass up this chance."

"When do you leave?" Dad asked the question everyone had to be wondering.

"Late spring approximately. We need to be there by June at the latest."

"So soon." Mom's words were a whisper.

"This is like an apprenticeship." Johanna had this all figured out. "How long will you be gone?"

"A year . . . maybe two. Alfred and Zach are still ironing out details. Some things are open-ended. Alfred has a large clientele and he's eager for Zach to come and work with him."

"And then you'll move back home to Colorado."

Payton and Zach had discussed how to answer this question. "Maybe . . . we don't know. We'll have to wait . . . pray . . . see what jobs are like."

Silence greeted her response. And then . . .

"We're excited for you, Zach." Beckett half stood and reached across the table to shake Zach's hand.

"Thanks. I appreciate it."

"It sounds terrific." Geoff clapped him on the back.

"I'm glad you two are so excited my sister is moving thousands of miles away." Jillian sniffled, her voice cracking.

"How are we going to do our Saturday morning book club now?" Johanna almost sounded angry.

Beckett settled back in his chair. "You told me you never even finished a book—"

"That's not the point, Beckett. We have a set time on the calendar every month to get together for coffee . . . and now it's ruined." Johanna pushed her chair away from the table. "I need to go check on Ellison."

"Jo—" Payton tried to catch her sister's hand as she rushed by, but Johanna ignored her. She glanced around the table at the rest of the family. "I'm sorry . . . we didn't mean to upset everyone . . ."

Zach pulled her close. "We're having to make plans. We don't like feeling as if we're keeping a secret from everyone."

"This family has had enough of those." Mom spoke first. "It's just a lot of change for Johanna. For all of us. First, we decide to move—a bit out of order, I admit. Buying a house before we've sold this one. And now you're moving . . ."

As Mom's voice trailed off, Dad took her hand. "What your mom is trying to say is we're glad you told us. It's going to take a little adjusting to—the idea of all of us here and you and Zach way over there in England."

"You are not helping, Don." Mom waved away his words, tears causing her voice to wobble.

"Sorry." Dad raised his hands in surrender. "Let me try again. We're all surprised. Just give us some time to adjust."

"We will. And now that you all know, we'll keep you updated on our plans—as much or as little as you want to know." Payton stood. "And now I think I'd better go find Johanna."

"Want me to go with you?" Jillian eased her chair back.

"Sure. You're always good at running interference when she's upset with me."

"Gladly."

Payton resisted the urge to link arms with Jillian. There was no need to present some show of sister-solidarity against Johanna. The three of them had grown past that kind of interaction in the past few years. They'd fought hard to find closeness with every Saturday morning book club where they drank coffee and talked about everything but books.

"I'm praying." Jillian's whisper reached her ears as they came to the foot of the stairs leading to the bedrooms.

"Me too. Keep it up."

"I will."

WHY COULDN'T ELLISON BE AWAKE? THEN JOHANNA could go inside the bedroom, pick up her daughter, and find comfort in snuggling her close. Savor the warmth of her body, the fresh scent of her hair from her bath last night, her sweet, "Hi, Mommy" breathed against her neck as Ellison transitioned from sleep to being awake.

Instead, here she sat in the semi-dark hallway scented by the too-cheery Christmas cookie candle in the nearby bathroom, hiding out from the rest of her family because she didn't want to go back and join the conversation.

She couldn't.

The low hum of voices reached her from the dining room, telling her that everyone was still discussing Payton and Zach's plans to move to England.

England!

Johanna closed her eyes and leaned against the wall. Why was everything changing? First Mom and Dad selling a perfectly good house. And now Payton and Zach moving thousands of miles away. And not a word said until everything was finalized.

Ridiculous.

"Joey, did you fall asleep up here?"

Jillian's question pulled Johanna upright. "What? No, I'm not asleep. I'm waiting for Ellison to wake up."

"Mind if we join you?" Jillian sat on the carpet on one side of her, Payton doing the same on the other side.

"Did you two tiptoe down the hallway?"

"No, but we were quiet in case Ellison was still asleep. Then we saw you sitting here with your eyes closed and we thought maybe you'd dozed off too."

"I was just thinking." Johanna sniffed, refusing to use the now-wadded-up tissue she'd taken from the bathroom when she first came upstairs.

"Are you crying?"

"I'm not crying." That was an honest statement. She wasn't crying *now*. And she'd only shed a few tears —of frustration—earlier.

"What's going on, Johanna?" Payton touched her arm.

"You tell me. You're the one moving to England."

"And you're mad about that because ..."

"I'm not mad." Johanna stared straight ahead, eyes focused on the wall across from her.

"You sound mad."

"Why are you changing everything?" Johanna still refused to make eye contact with either of her sisters.

"If there's one thing we've learned in the last three years, it's that life changes, Johanna."

"But we—the family has stayed together." Johanna fought to keep her voice from cracking. She was the unemotional one. "And now Mom and Dad are selling the house and you're moving ... and ... and ..."

"You expected Mom and Dad to always be in this house. And for the three of us to always be living close enough to meet once a month for our book club where we drink coffee and never read books."

"I really look forward to those Saturdays." Johanna, who was not crying, dabbed at her eyes with the useless tissue.

"We all do."

"Did I tell you ..." Oh why was she telling her sisters this? "Did I tell you that Beckett asked if we could move in together?"

Her question was greeted with silence for a moment—just space where she was heard, not judged.

"He did?" Payton responded first. "You two are moving forward then. That's good, right?"

"He wants us to buy a house together when his rental lease is up." Her shoulders shifted with a sigh that did nothing to ease the ache in her heart. "I told him no."

"You told him no . . . why?" Jillian slipped closer. "I thought things were going well between the two of you."

"They are . . . most days."

"But you don't want to move in with him?"

"No."

"We know your space is important to you, Jo." Payton turned to face her, but still allowed her space in the hallway.

"There's that . . . and I told him the house is the only home Ellison's known . . ."

"But?"

"After what Beckett and I went through . . . his cheating on me . . . I'm just wondering if living together gives him an out, you know?"

"What do you mean?"

"If we're not married, it's easier for him to cheat on me again."

"Married people cheat on each other too, Jo."

"I know . . . and you can call me old-fashioned . . . it just seems like there's more of a true commitment to marriage—"

"And you want that."

"Not that I'm going to tell Beckett."

"Why not?" Payton's words were edged with frustration.

"I'm not going to ask the man to marry me! And if he can't figure it out himself, then it just won't happen."

"Jo, come on." Jillian gave Johanna a half-hearted shake. "Help the guy out some. You know he loves you. I can see it—everyone sees it."

"I know he loves me—and he loves Ellison too. The question is, does he love me enough to marry me?"

"You're just going to let this go? Not talk it out?" Payton didn't want to push her sister, but she had to ask the question.

"I'm not a talker, Payton. You know that. I try . . . I've changed a lot in the past few years, haven't I?" Johanna waited as Jillian and Payton nodded in agreement. "Life doesn't look anything like I imagined it would by now . . . And yes, some of it is better than I expected. But with everything Beckett and I have been through, I don't think I should have to explain the difference between asking me to buy a house with him and asking me to marry him."

"Is there anything we can do, Jo?"

"No." As Ellison called for her, Johanna shifted and rose to her feet. "And now Ellison's awake."

"Thanks for talking, Johanna."

"Thanks for listening." Johanna paused with her hand on the doorknob. "Oh, there is one thing you can do."

"Name it."

"Don't talk to Beckett for me and try to fix this."

9

*T*he shuttle parking lot near the Broadmoor was more than half-full, and it was six o'clock on a Wednesday—which only proved the popularity of the Christmas lights display at Cheyenne Mountain Zoo. Even the chilly night air and temps dipping into the low thirties couldn't keep families away from the annual holiday tradition.

"I'm not sure this was a good idea." Johanna zipped Ellison's coat and then snugged her white hat with a fuzzy pom-pom down over her ears.

"Why not? She's been looking forward to seeing the Electric Safari all week." Beckett locked the car with a sharp electronic beep.

"She's been cranky today." Johanna searched for Ellison's mittens in the diaper bag. "I'm worried she's getting sick. Maybe we should have just stayed home—"

"She doesn't have a fever, does she?" Beckett lifted Ellison into his arms.

"No, I don't think so. I didn't check." Johanna pulled off her leather glove and pressed her fingers to Ellison's cheek, but it was cool to her touch. "Why didn't I take her temperature?"

"She's fine, Jo. We're not staying overnight. She'll love seeing the Christmas lights and the animals."

"See g-laffs, Daddy?" Ellison peered up at him, the edge of her hat pulled low over her eyes.

"Yes, sweetheart. You'll get to see the giraffes. And you can feed them too." He carried the stroller with one hand and nudged Johanna forward. "Let's go."

"We could have parked up at the zoo parking lot—"

"Maybe. Maybe not. I figured it was easier to park down here, take the shuttle up, and not worry about the traffic and whether we'd actually find a parking space at the zoo." He quickened his pace. "Come on. I see one of the shuttles pulling in."

But halfway to the shuttle, a man and a woman stepped out in front of them—and stopped. Johanna stumbled back. "Excuse me . . . *Jillian?*"

"Hello, Jo." Jillian gave an awkward half wave.

"And Geoff? What are you two doing here?"

"We came to see the Electric Safari . . . with our niece." Jillian reached for Ellison and Beckett handed her over. "Hey there, sweetie. Come give Aunt Jill a hug."

"What is going on?"

Beckett handed the stroller to Geoff. "Let Jillian have the diaper bag, Jo."

Johanna gripped the cloth straps. "Will someone tell me what is going on?"

"We're not going to see the zoo lights tonight, Jo—they are. And they need to hurry up and catch the shuttle." Beckett dug in his coat pocket. "Here are a spare set of keys so you can get the car seat and some cash for hot chocolate—whatever."

Geoff nodded. "We've got the food and souvenirs all covered. You two go have fun."

Jillian removed the diaper bag from Johanna's shoulder and gave her a quick hug. "Say bye-bye to Mommy and Daddy, Ellison, so we can go see the animals. Do you want to see the monkeys?"

"Yes!" Ellison grinned as she accepted a quick kiss from Johanna. "Bye, Mommy."

A few moments later, Johanna and Beckett stood in the parking lot as Jillian and Geoff disappeared with Ellison onto the waiting shuttle.

"Explain yourself." Johanna's demand was iced with cold air.

"I'm sorry if you wanted to see the zoo lights and animals, Jo. I planned something else for tonight."

"What?"

"A surprise." He took her hand and pulled her back toward the car. "Ready to go?"

"Where?"

"It's a surprise, remember?" He held the car door open, motioning for her to get in. "Do you trust me?"

Did she trust him? That was a very good question now, wasn't it?

"What time do we need to be back?" She fired the question off with a click of her seat belt.

"We don't have a curfew. Jillian and Geoff will take Ellison back to the house—I gave them the garage code—put her to bed, and then hang out until we get back." Beckett started the car, easing out of the space so that a waiting car could take their place.

"Are we going to dinner?"

"Are you hungry?"

Johanna stiffened. "Beckett, you know I don't like surprises and you've done that already tonight by handing our daughter off to Jill and Geoff—"

"I didn't give her to strangers." Beckett laughed. "And we have a two-year-old daughter, Jo. That means you've gotten much more flexible than you used to be because you've had to—we both have."

"I've had a stressful week. I'm not up for surprises tonight."

"Here." Beckett opened the console between the two seats and produced a Dove dark chocolate bar. "You're hungry."

"And now you're tossing food at me?"

"It's your favorite. And you just seem a little cranky—"

"Beckett!" Johanna twisted in the seat, pointing the candy bar at him. "What is going on?"

The man grinned. Tuned the radio to Christmas music. And then took her hand in his as he pulled up to a red light. "Chocolate. Patience. We'll be there soon enough."

She'd finished the chocolate and half the bottle of water Beckett gave her by the time he pulled the car into a small parking lot. Most of the shops looked closed except for a small Thai restaurant.

"You *are* feeding me."

"We're not eating here." Beckett came around to her side of the car and opened the door. He slipped his arm around her waist, guiding her to a small shop tucked into the corner of the line of storefronts, tapped on the oval-shaped glass etched with the words Edward Zimmerman, Jeweler.

Johanna stiffened. "What is this?"

"A jeweler's shop, obviously."

The door swung open. A wiry man with wavy black hair welcomed them with a smile. "Beckett! Right on time."

"Edward. Thank you for doing this." He took Johanna's hand and tugged her forward a few steps. "This is Johanna."

"Ah, yes. Johanna. What a pleasure to meet you at last." Edward shut the door and locked it before shaking her hand.

The jeweler's store was small, with the back curtained off, and contained only two glass cases, each with two shelves. One case displayed earrings and necklaces and a few brooches. The other exhibited rings, all against a backdrop of black velvet.

Johanna stood near the door. "This is your shop?"

"Yes. Please come in and look around." Edward motioned Johanna forward with a welcoming smile and a half bow. "I'll be in the back working on a Christmas gift for my wife if you have any questions."

And with those words, Edward disappeared behind the counter and into the back room.

Look around? At what?

"Exactly what is going on?" Johanna remained frozen by the locked front door.

Beckett, who had stayed calm all evening, scrubbed his hand down his face, his Adam's apple bobbing. He approached her, taking her hands in his. "This seemed . . . more romantic when I was planning it. I met Edward when I . . . when I was shopping for an engagement ring for you."

"An *engagement* ring?" Johanna tried to pull away, but Beckett refused to let go of her hands.

"Yes—but not the first time I bought you a ring. I came here a few weeks ago looking for a new ring for you. Edward asked me what you'd like . . . and I realized I didn't know." He stepped closer to her, pressing her hands to his chest, against his heart. "I want to get this proposal right, Johanna. The ring. The words . . . although I'm messing it up so badly already."

Johanna fought to speak past the tightening in her throat. "I thought . . . I thought you just wanted to buy a house. Move in together."

"I didn't want to push you. I thought that might be all you were ready for."

A thought zinged through Johanna's mind. "Did my sisters put you up to this?"

"What? No! I mean, I *did* call Jillian earlier this week and ask her if she could watch Ellison. But she and Payton don't know anything about the proposal." Beckett pressed his forehead to hers. "I love you, Johanna. I want to marry you. I want us to be a go-to-sleep-in-the same-house, wake-up-in-the-same-house, do-life-together-forever kind of family. Please . . . say yes even though I'm anything but perfect and I know I'm blowing this proposal."

"Oh, Beckett . . ." Johanna buried her face in the material of his coat.

His chest rose and fell with a deep sigh. "And if you can't say yes now . . . I'll wait . . ."

"Yes!" She grabbed his coat collar and pulled him closer, pressing a kiss to his lips. "Yes, Beckett Sager, I'll marry you. I want forever with you—for you and me and Ellison. Neither of us is perfect—but I love you so much."

Beckett wrapped his arms around her, his throaty laugh cut off as he kissed her. His lips were warm, his fingers caressing her skin as he pulled away and whispered her name before kissing her again.

"Everything okay out here—oh! Didn't mean to interrupt." Edward cleared his throat as he peered around the curtain.

Johanna hid her face in Beckett's shoulder.

"It's okay. I had to propose first before we could

look at the rings." He pressed a kiss to Johanna's cheek. "Shall we?"

"That would be wonderful. Maybe Edward could show us a few rings?"

"It would be my pleasure." The jeweler approached the glass case. "I have several custom designs, but as I told Beckett, I'm happy to design something for you, if that's more to your liking."

All thoughts of Edward designing an original ring for her vanished when Johanna saw an elegant emerald cut blue diamond framed by two bands of smaller diamonds positioned in the center of the case, set higher than any of the other rings. The white-gold band was also inlaid with diamonds.

"That's stunning."

"You told me she had impeccable taste, Beckett." Edward placed the ring on a black velvet stand on top of the case.

Beckett took Johanna's hand. "Shall we?"

"What are the odds it will actually fit?"

Beckett offered her a smile. "Maybe we'll have a little Christmas magic tonight."

"I'm no magician," Edward admitted, "but I can resize it for you within a few days if it doesn't fit."

But the ring slid on Johanna's finger as if Edward had designed it just for her. "It's perfect."

"Then it's the one."

"But we don't even know how much—"

"It's your ring, Jo." Beckett raised her hand to his lips and pressed a kiss to her palm, causing warmth to race up her arm. He offered her a quick wink. "Why don't you browse a little more while I settle with this gentleman? I may need to come back and do some Christmas shopping."

A few minutes later as they exited the shop, Beckett whispered, "Happy?"

"I'm almost completely, perfectly happy."

"Almost?" He stopped. "I know. You're hungry."

"Well, there is that. But there's actually one more thing . . ."

"Name it."

"JOHANNA! BECKETT! I DIDN'T EXPECT TO SEE YOU tonight." Mom stepped back from the front door to allow them to enter. "Is everything all right?"

"Yes." Joanna held on to Beckett's hand even as she gave Mom a quick half-hug. "We took Ellison to see the zoo lights tonight."

"Ellison? Where is she?" Mom peered around them, as if her granddaughter might be walking up the front walkway by herself.

"Actually, Beckett made plans for Jillian and Geoff to take Ellison to the zoo lights." Johanna stepped inside her parents' home, Beckett following her. "Is Dad still up?"

"Yes. We were watching *It's a Wonderful Life* while I worked on my Christmas cards."

Johanna slipped off her coat. "I still can't convince

you to go with electronic Christmas cards, can I?"

"No. I enjoy sending out real ones—even if some of my friends have gone the virtual route." Mom hugged Beckett as they placed their coats on the banister railing leading upstairs. "Do you want some coffee?"

Johanna exchanged a quick glance with Beckett. "Sure. We wanted to talk with you and Dad about something—if you don't mind us interrupting your movie."

"No, no, that's all right."

"Did I hear Johanna and Beckett?" Dad appeared at the top of the stairs leading to the family room.

"Hi, Dad." Johanna moved forward and gave him a hug. "Everything's fine. We just dropped by because we wanted to talk to you and Mom about something. Jillian and Geoff took Ellison to the zoo lights."

Mom motioned toward the kitchen. "I'll get the coffee. Do you want some, Don?"

"Only if I can have some of your homemade divinity." He followed Mom into the kitchen. "Why don't we just adjourn to the breakfast nook?"

It didn't take long for Mom to set a plate of divinity in the middle of the table. A candle scented the air with the spicy aroma of gingerbread. "Well, this is nice. Did you have a good date night?"

"Yes." Johanna held Beckett's hand beneath the table. "It's been a wonderful evening."

"I bet you don't get too many date nights." Dad selected a piece of divinity and sipped his coffee.

"Did you go out for dinner?"

"No . . . we got a bit distracted."

"Distracted?" Mom took a small piece of her home-made confection.

"Yes. Beckett distracted me with this." Johanna slipped her hand from Beckett's and held it up, revealing her diamond.

Mom gasped. "Johanna! You're engaged!"

"I am. I'm engaged." Johanna paused to catch her breath. "Beckett arranged everything with Jillian and Geoff so he could take me to this wonderful custom jeweler's shop and propose—and then we selected this ring."

Mom took her hand, twisting it back and forth so the light caused the diamonds to sparkle. "This is such a beautiful ring. I'm so happy for you—for all three of you."

Dad reached across the table and shook Beckett's hand. "Well done, son. That's quite a proposal story."

"And now we have to plan a wedding." Mom stopped. "Are you going to get married before Payton and Zach move overseas?"

"We talked about that on the drive here and yes, that's what we'd like to do."

"Johanna also had one other caveat to our getting married." Beckett took her hand again. "And I completely agreed with her."

"She did? What?"

"Mom . . . Dad . . . Beckett and I would like to buy your house."

"Our house? *This house?*" Mom set her coffee cup down on the table with a soft thud.

"Yes. This house." Johanna leaned forward. "I love this house. The location is wonderful. It's larger than my house—"

"Which is perfect for us, since we most likely will be expanding our family in the future." Beckett winked at Johanna.

"We love the layout and the backyard and it's a good school district. And most of all, I love that this home represents our family."

"Johanna . . . I never realized . . ."

"I never realized it either. Not until you and Dad decided to sell the house." Johanna blinked away the threat of tears. "To be honest, Beckett and I may make some design changes to the house in the future— update the kitchen, maybe put in new flooring. Would you be okay with that?"

"The bigger question is, would they be okay if we bought the house?" Beckett glanced back and forth between Mom and Dad. "Then we can discuss the other things."

"What do you think, Don?"

"I think it's a wonderful idea." Dad rubbed his hands together, nodding his head. "Of course, we'd still need to work with our Realtor—do this right."

"Of course. We know what you and Mom are asking for the house and we want to offer that—"

"We can discuss that. The important thing is we don't cut out Tracey because a family member is buying the house. We do all the normal things—a house inspection, the home warranty plan we were offering, and we also decide on a closing date that works for the four of us."

"Absolutely." Beckett nodded. "We wouldn't want this any other way."

"And once you own the house, it's yours." Mom smiled. "You can change things around. Knock down walls . . . whatever."

Johanna hesitated for a moment. And then—"So we have a deal?"

"Yes. Shall we shake on it?" Mom grinned.

"How about a hug?" Johanna stood, stepping into Mom's embrace. "It's been quite the night. First Beckett and I get engaged and then we decide to buy a house."

"Sounds like Christmas came early for you this year."

"It did, didn't it?"

10

*J*t was the Sunday before Christmas, and the entire family was unpacking and then repacking Christmas. Johanna had coordinated the event, purchasing new boxes and multicolored Sharpies—red for Payton, blue for Jillian, green for Johanna, and orange for Mom and Dad. All they had to do was show up at the set time and be ready to work. Mom promised to feed all of them, while Dad promised to entertain Ellison upstairs with a holiday movie.

"It's odd to be sorting through all the Christmas decorations, instead of decorating the house this year." Payton removed a container of lights from a box. "At least you and Dad are organized."

"Organized, yes, but there's still so much to do." Mom stood, hands on her hips, surveying all the boxes marked ORNAMENTS. "I need to know which ones you and your sisters want to keep."

"Shouldn't you and Dad decide first?"

"We discussed it last night. There are a few ornaments we want to keep, like the ones your dad gave me on our wedding anniversaries, but the three of you are free to choose from the other ones and keep whichever ones you want."

"Do you think we can do that without bickering?" Payton plugged the lights into the wall. When the lights turned on, she unplugged them and set them off to the side.

"You're all adults. I'm sure you'll be able to handle this without it becoming too stressful." Mom selected a handmade felt ornament shaped like a bell. "I assume you'll want any ornaments Pepper made."

"Some of them, yes. But you and Dad might want some too—or maybe Jill or Jo. And I'm fine with that."

"What do you want to do with some of these generic decorations, Mom?" Johanna interrupted their conversation, carrying a medium-sized plastic box down the stairs, Beckett following behind her with another box in his arms. "These are marked 'Coordinated ornaments.' I think there are only a few more boxes in the attic."

"Oh, those are from the years when I tried to match the lights and the colors on the tree. That only lasted for two or three years. If no one wants them, let's just give them away."

"The giveaway pile it is."

"That pile keeps growing, doesn't it?" Mom's voice held a hint of laughter.

"That's the goal, right? You're moving and downsizing." Johanna pointed to an artificial tree, still in its box, while the much smaller Realtor-approved tree stood in the living room window. "Do you still want this?"

"No, that's a giveaway item too. I forgot we still had that." Mom shook her head. "We should probably just throw it out. We haven't used it in years, and your dad and I decided we'd continue with the smaller Christmas tree in our new house."

"No live tree?" Johanna's eyes widened.

"No. The three of you can keep that tradition going, but your dad and I are opting for a fake tree from now on."

"Did you see these, Mom?" Jillian knelt beside a box, an assortment of ornaments spread on the carpet in front of her, and held up a small felt ornament. "Look at my pigtails."

Payton sat beside her, Johanna and Mom standing behind them as Jillian handed Mom a handmade ornament featuring a photograph of Jillian's smiling face.

"Oh my! You were probably in first grade, Jill." Mom's laughter was tinged with tears.

"Look at me! Mom, did you keep all of our school ornaments?" Johanna traced the gold plastic rim surrounding her school photo before showing it to Payton.

"Of course! Just because I stopped putting them on

the tree—you all put up such a fuss about them—didn't mean I threw them out."

Payton selected an ornament of two connected pink hearts. One had the name Pepper written on it. The other was inscribed with the name Payton. "I'm definitely hanging this on my tree this year." She glanced at Mom. "Is that okay?"

"Absolutely." More tears welled in Mom's eyes. "I remember how you both used to fight to hang that on the Christmas tree when you were younger. Your dad always helped you and Pepper because we didn't want it to get broken."

"No one touch any of my Broncos ornaments!" Dad's warning from the top of the stairs caused everyone to laugh.

"We didn't realize you were there." Mom rose to meet him as he carried Ellison down into the room.

"The movie ended, and Ellison wanted to see what was going on."

"I can hold her." Mom shifted Ellison onto her hip.

"Dad, you could have an entire Bronco themed tree." Jillian grinned at her suggestion.

"That's not a bad idea."

"Absolutely not." Mom's veto was swift.

"How about a small one—in my study in the new house?"

"I'll think about it."

"Mom, Dad, . . . I don't think I've ever asked this before—do you have any ornaments from your families?" Payton half turned so she could see both her parents.

"No." Dad's answer was quick. "When my parents died, well, the relatives got into a bit of wrangling about who got what. I didn't care for any of that nonsense, so I just backed off and let them have it."

"Oh, Dad. I'm sorry."

"It's just stuff, Pay. Not worth arguing about."

"What about you, Mom?"

Mom's gaze shifted away, even as she rubbed gentle circles on Ellison's back.

"Mom?"

"Oh . . . sorry." Mom shook her head, as if dismissing a thought. "I was thinking about what Christmas was like growing up. We moved a lot. My father was always looking for 'the next big thing.' That's what he always told us—life was about the next big thing. He tried all sorts of jobs. Sometimes we were even on the road on Christmas Day. One year, we moved so quickly we left a lot of our stuff behind—including my mom's Christmas ornaments. I still remember how hard she cried when she realized that. Of course, we couldn't go back and get them."

"Oh, Mom . . . I'm so sorry." Payton wished she could hug her, but Mom still held Ellison.

"So . . . to answer your question . . . no, I don't have any of my family's Christmas ornaments."

"And that's why you always make Christmas so special for us." Jillian offered Payton a hug, even as she smiled at Mom.

"Well, I hope you all have wonderful memories of Christmas together, and I'm sorry this Christmas has been a bit hectic."

"We do—and we'll make new ones in your new home next year." Payton closed the lid on the container of lights. "And Christmas is still special, even with packing up and moving."

"Yes. We're all together." Jillian hugged Dad.

"That's the best gift of all."

"It is." Jillian nodded in agreement.

"I'm sorry the offer fell through on your house, but you can get it back on the market after New Year's—" Payton rose to her feet, dusting her hands off on the front of her jeans.

"Well, that was going to be our Christmas surprise for you all—" Mom looked at Dad and raised her eyebrows.

"What? Did the people who made you that cash offer come back? I wouldn't trust those buyers again—"

"No, but we did get another offer and we accepted it."

"How?" Jillian spoke up. "You and Dad took the house off the market—didn't you?"

"This was an unusual offer . . ."

"Who's buying the house?"

"Beckett and I are." Johanna put her arm around Beckett's waist.

"What?" Payton and Jillian spoke in unison.

"When I proposed, Johanna wouldn't say yes unless we also bought this house."

"Proposed?" Payton focused on Beckett. "When did you propose?"

"Where's your ring?" Jillian rushed Johanna, grabbing her hand.

"Give me a minute." Johanna laughed as Jillian hugged her. "I took it off when we were driving over. If I came in wearing it, you and Payton would have noticed it right away."

As Jillian stepped back, Beckett removed a ring from his pants pocket and slipped it on Johanna's left ring finger and then raised her hand while leaning in for a kiss. "Back where it belongs."

"Agreed. No more taking it off."

"How long have you kept this a secret?"

"Not a secret, really. Thatchers don't keep secrets anymore. We wanted to surprise you—to tell you and Jillian together about the proposal and that we're buying Mom and Dad's house."

"Why?" Payton accepted Zach's hand and stood, brushing off her hands.

"Why am I marrying this guy? About time, don't you think?"

"No—why are you buying the house?"

"Because this is where we want Ellison to grow up. If you think about it, this is the perfect house. The size. The location. But most of all, the memories tucked inside these walls make all the difference."

"Jo—" Payton came and embraced Johanna, Jillian

joining her for a triple embrace. The scent of Johanna's favorite Chanel perfume wrapped around them. Had she ever shed happier tears with her sisters?

"We may change things some. You two okay with that?"

"Of course. Make this your home."

Payton nodded at Jillian's words, clearing the tightness in her throat. "We can hold on to the memories even as you make new ones."

"Speaking of making memories, let's not forget we promised Ellison that we're all going to see the Christmas lights tonight." Dad's words had us all nodding.

Mom added a fourth to our hug. "And I'll remember to make some hot chocolate and popcorn, as she requested."

"And then tomorrow, we have our annual Christmas symphony concert," Johanna reminded us.

"While the men babysit Ellison and spend the day together eating chili." Dad grinned as Beckett and Zach cheered. "One of my favorite family holiday traditions."

"I'll never be too old to go looking at Christmas lights." I settled back into the passenger seat as Don turned back onto the main road, happy that he was cleared to drive once again after his surgery. "That last neighborhood had a lot of nice houses."

"I like the old-fashioned, multi-colored lights."

"You say that every year." I patted his hand where it rested on the steering wheel.

"And I mean it every year too. I'm just not a fan of the LED lights." Don eased to a stop behind Johanna and Beckett's car.

"Every generation has a new take on Christmas lights."

"I guess so. Where to now?"

At his question, my cell phone rang. "That would be Johanna, directing the caravan."

Don motioned toward my phone when it rang again. "Aren't you going to answer it?"

I ignored the phone. "I had an idea—"

"Of where to go next to look at lights?"

"Well, yes and no. I was thinking maybe we could go look at the new house with everyone."

"That would be nice."

The phone went silent for a few brief moments and then started ringing again.

Don motioned toward the phone as he pulled into the intersection. "Go ahead and suggest it. It's not too far from here and the family might like the idea."

I connected the call. "Hello, Johanna."

"Why didn't you answer the first time, Mom?"

"Dad and I were talking."

"Okay. Well, I was thinking we could go—"

"That's what we were talking about—where we could go next."

There was silence on the other end of the phone for a second. "Really? Where do you want to go?"

"We're not that far from our new house—maybe ten minutes. Dad and I thought we could drive there so everyone could see it."

"But it's dark—we won't be able to see all that much."

"I hadn't really thought about that . . . I was just excited to drive by the house and show everyone the neighborhood since we're all together." Johanna's practicality muted my excitement. I swallowed the urge to repeat the request. "Never mind. It wasn't a good idea."

"Wait, Mom. Let's do it." Johanna's voice had softened. "I'll text Payton and Jill and tell them what we're doing. You and Dad lead the way, but go ahead and text us all the address, in case we get separated."

After a short drive, our little caravan pulled up in front of our home-to-be. Johanna was correct, there wasn't much to see. While surrounding houses were decorated for Christmas, the windows warmed from within with lights, our house stood dark, the Realtor sign with its Under Contract attachment posted in the yard.

Everyone lined up on the sidewalk, Ellison snug in Beckett's arms with Johanna next to him, Payton next to Zach, and then Jillian and Geoff completing the family group.

"Here it is." Don swept his arm wide.

"It's nice. I like the big windows." Zach spoke first.

"They're brand new."

"I can imagine that little Christmas tree positioned right in the front window next year, Mom." Johanna spoke next. "But with all your ornaments, not just white lights. It'll look beautiful."

"And there's a small fireplace in the family room area, so we can put up everyone's stockings."

"So . . . this is where we'll be celebrating Christmas next year," Johanna announced.

"Or maybe the family can come to England for Christmas." Payton's voice was tentative.

"Ooh! A Christmas in merry old England!" Jillian clapped her hands, the sound muffled by her mittens.

"That's certainly worth considering—a whole new Christmas tradition for the Thatcher family." Don pulled me close. "What do you think, my dear?"

"I love the idea." I blinked back tears, which seemed to come so easily these days. "I'm so excited about what the next year holds for us. For all of us."

"But first, we've got to move into this house."

"And Beckett and I have to get married."

"And Zach and I have to get to England."

"But the very first thing we all have to do," Jillian interrupted us, "is celebrate Christmas in less than a week."

With hugs and wishes of Merry Christmas, we all piled back into our cars and went our separate ways. Don waited as everyone else drove off.

"This was a good idea, coming to see the house."

"Thanks. It makes it all a little more real." I took a sip of tepid hot chocolate.

"Happy?"

"About the house? Yes. You?"

"Very happy." Don reached for my hand.

"But it's more than that—"

"What do you mean?"

"For the first time in years . . . I'm not scared about the future. I should be, especially with what happened to you in the last two weeks." I twisted to face Don. "I'm just leaning into all the reasons I'm thankful. You're still here. The girls are happy and everyone is living their lives, even if there are struggles. And isn't that what we want for our children?"

"Yes."

"The girls are closer than they've ever been—and I don't think Payton and Zach moving overseas will change that. I'm glad we sold the house, Don. I realize now that growing up the way I did made me afraid of change. My dad's way of life? Nothing ever felt stable. The truth is, we should have sold the house sooner."

Don offered me a smile, his eyes full of understanding. "It's okay, Heather."

"Watching the girls work through so much these past few years is helping me see it's okay to change. To let go of the past and step into the future. Selling the house is part of that."

"After all this time, are you telling me that you're glad I suggested selling the house?"

"I guess I am." I leaned across the console and shared a kiss with my husband. "You're a very smart man, Don Thatcher."

"I married you, didn't I?" He winked as he started the car. "Shall we head home?"

"Yes. Tomorrow we can put presents under the tree."

"Oh—that reminds me. I have a little shopping to finish up."

"Don! It's the week before Christmas."

"I know, I know. But you have to admit life was a little interrupted this month."

"I can come with you—"

"Not this time." He pulled away from the curb. "Sometimes a husband has a few Christmas surprises, you know."

"Oh, really?"

"Yes, really. And that's all I'm going to say about that. No more questions, Mrs. Thatcher."

11

*C*hristmas morning was quiet, but what did Jillian expect when it was only the two of them—three, if she counted Winston. Yes, she had added a small red *Winston* stocking to the mantel in their living room, which was also decorated with a modest nativity scene and two other stockings stitched with *Jillian* and *Geoff*. Jillian had filled Winston's stocking with a bag of his favorite doggy treats and a new squeaky toy, while resisting the reindeer ears that Winston would have shaken off within a matter of seconds.

Now Winston slept curled up at the foot of the couch on the soft green Christmas blanket decorated with snowflakes. The aroma of fresh-baking cinnamon rolls scented the air. She and Geoff had finished opening their few presents to one another, saying all the appropriate, appreciative comments.

It was a good morning. Geoff had given her a gift

card for monthly facials at a local salon, as well as a new sweater and a bottle of her favorite perfume.

He'd seemed to like her coupon for scuba lessons —continuing with the "let's have fun" theme—and a new coat.

Jillian shifted on the couch where she and Geoff still relaxed together. "I should check on the cinnamon rolls and then we can get ready—"

"Wait." Geoff placed a hand on her wrist to stop her from standing. "I have one more gift for you."

"What?" Jillian scanned the area around the tree. "We've opened everything."

"It's here." Geoff leaned away as he stretched and pulled a small ornament from within the tree, causing the tree branches to shake a little.

"An ornament. That's so sweet . . ."

"Open it."

"Open it?" As Geoff placed it in her hands, Jillian realized the ornament was hinged, decorated to look like a Christmas present wrapped in red paper and decorated with a gold bow.

It only took a small bit of pressure to open the box. Inside was a tiny slip of paper. "What's this?"

Geoff nodded. "Go ahead and read it."

Jillian set the ornament in her lap, unfolded the paper, and read the words *Let's talk*.

Let's talk.

"Merry Christmas, Jill." Geoff offered her a smile, his eyes lit with a warm glow behind his glasses.

"I . . . I don't understand."

Geoff took her hands, easing closer to her. "That's my Christmas gift to you—I want to talk about children. You and me . . . and having children."

"What?" Her fingers trembled as she held on to the slip of paper.

"You've been so patient with me . . . loved me enough to table the conversation about starting a family for two years. I want you to know that I love you enough to go to counseling and start the conversation with you about having a family together—"

"What changed your mind?"

"I talked with Brian a couple of times. First, he told me how stubborn I'm being, refusing to go to counseling with you and talk this issue out."

"He said you're being stubborn, huh?" Jillian tried to hide her smile.

"Yeah. And then he also told me that I'm scared. That hit home the most—because he's right. I am scared."

"Oh, Geoff . . ."

"The truth is, Jill, you're the brave one, not me. I'm amazed how you keep going with all you face, day in and day out, since you had cancer—"

"You help me face it, Geoff. You and my faith."

Geoff pulled Jillian close so she could rest her head on his shoulder. "I love you, Jill—so much. I don't think it will be easy to talk about all this—as a matter of fact, Brian warned me it would be tough. But I'm willing to try."

"I know this doesn't mean we're going to have children or adopt." She tried to ignore the sharp twinge in her chest caused by her words. "We'll find a counselor we both like and talk this out. We'll listen to each other."

"Merry Christmas, Jill." Geoff's words were like a warm caress against her skin.

"Merry Christmas, Geoff." Jill closed her fingers around the treasured slip of paper. "I love you."

"I know you do." Geoff rested his chin on top of her head. "Thank you for being patient with me."

"Thank you for loving me enough to risk this."

Instead of rushing to get ready to go to her parents', Jillian sat in her husband's embrace and savored the new common ground they'd found on Christmas morning—because they'd chosen to love each other enough.

"WHERE'S DAD?" PAYTON ASKED THE QUESTION I'D wondered myself.

"He said he had one more present for me." I shrugged. "I can't imagine what it could be."

"The wooden table he made with Zach's help is beautiful."

I ran my fingertips over the small side table Don had given me earlier this morning. "I'm impressed. I don't think your dad has ever done any woodworking."

"Dad's a natural." Zach grinned. "He said he'd like

to do some more projects if we can fit them in before I go to England."

"Is this . . . this what you were working on when Dad collapsed?"

"Yes. It was mostly finished—"

"He told me that you had to complete it for him, but this explains why he disappeared a couple of Saturdays this fall."

"Surprises are always fun."

And now the table was all the more precious when I recalled how I feared I might lose Don the day he collapsed.

"Speaking of surprises, where is he?"

"Right here." Don took the stairs down into the family room one careful step at a time. "Merry Christmas, Heather."

Don bent over and released a small white bundle of fur adorned with a red bow that wiggled and yipped . . . and then plopped down at his feet.

I blinked my eyes. "Is that . . . *a puppy*?"

"She's your puppy . . . your Christmas puppy."

"Don!" His name came out on a half-gasp and half-laugh.

He scooped my present up and deposited it . . . her . . . in my lap. "What do you think?"

"I think you're crazy! We're moving into a new house . . . the last thing we need is a puppy!" I scratched underneath her chin as she snuggled in my arms. "Oh, she's so soft. Where did you get her?"

"Santa brought her, of course." Don laughed—

such a wonderful sound. "Believe it or not, I've been looking online at the animal shelter for a few months and found her there. She's been staying at Payton and Zach's this week until she could come home . . ."

"You all knew I was getting a puppy?" Guilty smiles greeted my question. "I know this is going to be your dog just as much as it's going to be mine, Don."

"If you want to share her, I won't complain. We can train her together—"

"What is Winston going to think?"

"He'll enjoy having a new playmate." Jillian seemed as happy as her dad about the new canine addition to the family.

"Even more important, what are you going to call her?" Johanna, ever the practical one.

"I have no idea." I tipped my head and inhaled the warm scent of new puppy.

"You could name her Marshmallow because she's white." Johanna pulled out her phone and began looking up possible names.

"Or Snowball."

"Or Frosty."

"What about Bailey?" Don readjusted the bow as the puppy tried to chew it.

"Bailey?" I tilted my head.

"After the Bailey family in *It's a Wonderful Life*."

"Hi, Bailey." I snuggled the puppy close so that we were nose to wet nose, laughing when she whimpered. "You like that name? Welcome to the family, Bailey."

EPILOGUE
SATURDAY, JANUARY 8, 2022

"The first book club meeting of the new year." Johanna settled on the couch, tucking her feet underneath her. She shifted, pulling out a small plastic duck from behind her, giving it a little squeeze so that it quacked. "Didn't see that before I sat down."

"What is Beckett doing with Ellison this morning?" Payton sat at the other end of the couch.

"Going out for a daddy-daughter breakfast."

"That sounds like fun."

"He tries to do it once a month or so." Johanna sipped her coffee. "So . . . how are we all doing?"

"Good." Jillian spoke first. "Geoff and I are trying to find a counselor so we can start the do-we-or-don't-we-have-children discussion."

"How do you feel about that, Jilly?"

"Hopeful. Thankful." She sighed. "I've waited for this for so long—just the opportunity to talk about children . . . this is good. It's forward motion."

"I'm happy for you." Payton reached over and clasped her hand. "Prayers answered."

"Some of them, anyway. We'll see what happens in the future."

"You two realize we've got a busy six months ahead of us, right?" Johanna raised her hand and began ticking off items. "Beckett and I will be closing on Mom and Dad's house. Then we need to sell my house. They'll be moving. We'll be moving. There's my wedding to plan. And last but definitely not least, Payton and Zach's move overseas. Did I miss anything?"

"Just the usual birthdays and anniversaries." Jillian offered a salute with a grin. "This year is going to be memorable, that's for sure—and that's just the first six months."

"What kind of wedding do you want, Jo?"

"Small. Family and a few friends." How could she explain to her sisters that she didn't miss her original plan for a grand wedding? "Dot and Axton even volunteered their home."

"Are you considering that?"

"Their home is lovely, so yes, it would work, but I'm also thinking about a mountain location—maybe Aspen or Vail. We could take a long weekend."

"That would be nice too." Jillian leaned forward. "What kind of ceremony are you thinking of?"

"I'm not, actually." Johanna set her coffee aside. "Beckett and I have talked about it and we want just our family there. A few friends. But when it comes to the ceremony, we want it to be just us—Beckett and me and whoever marries us."

"And who do you want to do that?"

"Of course, we don't have a minister or anyone like that. We're not looking for a church service." Johanna paused. "And you can have anyone marry you in Colorado."

"That's true."

"We were thinking of asking Zach."

"*Zach*?" Payton sat up straight, her blue-green eyes wide. "Why Zach?"

"Beckett and Zach get along—well, Zach gets along with everyone. And we think he'd respect what we believe . . . what we *don't* believe. You've both been good about that. We'd probably write our own vows. What do you think, Payton?"

"I think . . . I think Zach would be honored. Do you want me to ask him?"

"You can mention it to him—let him know we're thinking about it but that we haven't decided anything definite. If we decide that's what we want, we'll ask him."

"I've been thinking about something." Jillian pulled her legs up, wrapping her arms around them and resting her chin on top of her knees.

"What?"

"About keeping our not-a-book-club going via FaceTime or Zoom once Payton is living in England—if you two want to, that is."

"I think that's a wonderful idea!" Payton's smile backed up her words.

"I do too."

"I also thought we could invite someone else—"

"Someone else? Who?" Johanna frowned.

"Mom."

Payton clapped. "Why didn't we think of that sooner?"

"I have no idea. Who knows, with Mom a part of our group, we just might read a book or two."

"We're in agreement then? We're inviting Mom to join our book club?"

Johanna raised her coffee cup. "I vote yes."

Payton mirrored her movement. "I vote yes."

"That makes three of us—and I suggest we invite her to join us next month. Why wait until Payton moves to England?"

Their "Hear! Hear!" blended into a beautiful chorus of sister laughter.

THE END

DISCUSSION QUESTIONS

1. What surprised you the most about how life has changed for the Thatcher sisters, Johanna, Jillian, and Payton, since you'd last connected with them in *The Best We've Been*? If you haven't read the other three novels in the series yet, what surprised you the most in *Unpacking Christmas*?

2. What did you learn about the Thatcher sisters' parents that helped you understand Johanna, Jillian, and Payton better?

3. Do your parents still live in the house where you grew up? If they do, what are your feelings about that? If they've sold the house, what kind of feelings did you have about not being able to go back to your childhood home? Some adult children are buying their childhood homes and renovating them for their families—there

are even TV shows about this. Would you ever buy your parents' home? Why or why not?

4. Have you ever moved during the Christmas holiday season? What kind of challenges did you face? Or maybe you moved during the school year—what was your experience like?

5. Payton and Zach surprised the family with a change of their own when they announced they were moving overseas. How do you feel about living so far away from family and missing all the traditional family get-togethers and celebrations? Would you embrace a change like that or choose to stay close to family?

6. At the end of *Unpacking Christmas*, Jillian and Geoff have decided to discuss whether they're going to try to start a family—either through in vitro fertilization or through adoption. Every married couple faces tough topics they need to navigate through. Friendships do too. What helps you talk through things with someone you love?

7. Jillian and Beckett's relationship has changed—improved—since book three, *The Best We've Been*. What are your thoughts about where they ended up at the end of *Unpacking Christmas*? Is there anything you would have changed?

8. Johanna, Jillian, and Payton each have a different faith journey through the series (*Things I Never Told You*; *Moment We Forget*; *The Best We've Been*). Why do you think the author wrote the sisters' journeys the way she did? How would you change them?

ACKNOWLEDGMENTS

"Not to us, O LORD, not to us, but to Thy name give glory, because of Thy lovingkindness, because of Thy truth." (Psalm 115 NASB)

Unpacking Christmas is my first venture into self-publishing. After the chaos of 2020 disrupted my writing life, I determined to rediscover my creativity in 2021. Writing a Christmas novella seemed like a wonderful way to dive back into story again. Revisiting the Thatcher sisters has been so much fun, and I'm thankful so many readers have asked me about them since the third book in the series, *The Best We've Been*, was published in 2020.

My family was, as always, the best support as I focused on Christmas through winter, spring, and summer 2021. I couldn't pursue my writing dream without their understanding and encouragement. Let's be honest, I rarely cook dinner anymore. I love you, one and all. Family is the best.

I had Rachel Hauck on speed-dial through this entire process. Most people probably know her as a best-selling author, but to me she's a trusted friend, mentor, brainstormer, and prayer warrior – not to mention my go-to person whenever I had questions about self-publishing. When I called and told her that I was changing the initial novella idea to a Thatcher sisters' story, she said, "I told you that months ago!" Yes, she had – and she was right.

My morning prayer group-via-text is made up of talented writer-friends who encourage me daily: Lisa Jordan, Alena Tauriainen, Melissa Tagg, Susan May Warren, Tari Faris, and Rachel Hauck – I'm so thankful our relationships are woven together with prayer.

For every time you've asked me, "How's your heart?" – thank you, Kristy Cambron. Thank you.

Edie Melson, my day starts off with a text from you and the question, "How can I pray for you?" And that makes such a difference in how my day goes. Thank you, my friend. Thank you. You inspire me.

Mary Agius, I couldn't do the writing life without all our brainstorming walks and you asking, "What about . . .?" To be honest, our walks and talks enrich my life.

My wonderful cover that so beautifully captures *Unpacking Christmas* was designed by the talented Hillary Manton Lodge. Thank you, Hillary, for fitting me in your already full schedule. Barbara Curtis, you're a stellar line editor – thank you for those smiley faces. And Lianne March, I'm so grateful Rachel Hauck recommended you as an editor. You did a wonderful job proofing my manuscript.

Lindsay Harrel, thank you so much for formatting my manuscript for me. For you? It's easy. For me? It's magic!

Thank you, Angie Arndt, for your beautiful creativity in designing the logo for Never Door Press. It's perfect.

Jan Stob, my trusted editor at Tyndale House Publishing, thanks for supporting this "what's happening with the Thatcher sisters?" novella. I loved working with you on the first three novels.

Thank you, Rachelle Gardner, for being my agent as I embraced being a hybrid author. Here's to where the writing road leads next!

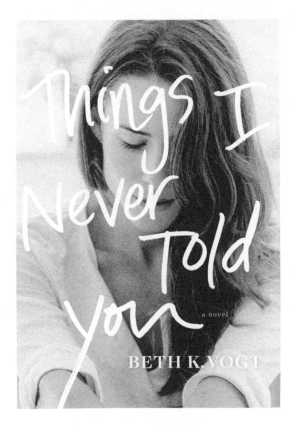

Interested in finding out how the award-winning Thatcher Sisters Series began? Read the first chapter of *Things I Never Told You*, book one in Beth K. Vogt's "'*Little Women*' gone wrong" series. Turn the page for a sneak peek ...

The what-ifs taunted me every time I visited my parents, but any hope of beginning again had vanished years ago—if there'd ever been one.

What would have happened if my parents had gone through with selling the house in Colorado Springs my sisters and I had grown up in? If they'd labeled and taped up all the boxes—the clothes, the books, the dishes, the photographs, the awards, and the trophies—and unpacked them in a different house?

A change of location. A chance to start over.

But unexpected loss held my parents captive.

For the most part, our family seemed unchanged. The kitchen clock—a porcelain plate decorated with bright red-and-yellow flowers but lacking any numerals to designate the passing of time—hung in the same place it had since a dozen Mother's Days ago.

The same white wooden shutters hid the bay windows in the breakfast nook. The same worn round table in the middle, surrounded by four chairs adorned with nondescript blue cushions our mother changed out every few years—whenever Johanna reminded her to do so.

I pushed the Start button on the once-new dishwasher. My parents had installed it at the Realtor's recommendation when they'd planned to move into the larger house that offered a coveted view of Pikes Peak.

Time to focus on the cheesecakes—the engagement party dessert finale. The hum of the dishwasher blended with garbled conversation as the door between the kitchen and dining room opened, the sound of Jillian's fiancé's booming laughter sneaking in. Geoff and his corny jokes.

"Just getting the dessert, Kim—"

"I'm not your timekeeper, little sister." Johanna's no-nonsense voice interrupted my concentration.

I stiffened, gripping the handles of the fridge. Why hadn't I posted a Do Not Enter sign on the door? Maybe I should have caved to Nash's insistence to attend the party, even though tonight was more work than play for me. Why not have my boyfriend act as bouncer outside the kitchen? Flex his muscles and run interference?

I had no time for my oldest sister. Any minute now, Kimberlee would return from setting up the silver carafes of coffee and hot water for tea, along with cream, sugar, spoons, and other necessities. She'd expect the trio of cheesecakes to be arranged on their individual stands—my job tonight, since we'd only had the caterers deliver the food for such a small gathering.

"Do you need something, Johanna?" I pulled the first cheesecake from the fridge, my mouth watering at the thought of key lime and dollops of whipped cream. Being the party planner for tonight meant I'd had no chance to indulge in the hors d'oeuvres or cocktails, despite this being my other sister's engagement party. And vegan or not, I could appreciate a decadent dessert—and postpone interacting with Johanna.

"You and Kimberlee are pretty good at this event-planning business." Johanna leaned against the kitchen counter.

"Mom and Jillian seem happy. That's the important thing." I settled the cheesecake on its stand, the plastic wrap clinging to my fingers as I uncovered it. "It's all about finding out what people want and then making it happen."

"Festivities is making enough to pay the bills, apparently."

"Yes."

Not that I was going to produce an Excel spread-sheet of our accounts payable and receivable for my oldest sister.

"You two didn't charge Mom and Dad full price—"

"Really, Johanna?" Not sparing my sister a glance, I

shoved the fridge door closed with my hip, a turtle cheesecake balanced in my hands.

"Oh, don't get in a huff, Payton. Honestly, how do you manage your customers if you're so touchy?"

And this . . . this was yet another reason why I didn't come home unless absolutely necessary. I concentrated on transporting the second cheesecake from the fridge to the island, refusing to square off with my sister. Best to change the subject and prep the desserts.

"Jillian and Geoff seem perfect for one another, don't they?"

Johanna took the bait. "Of course they do. They enjoy the same foods. The same movies. He makes her laugh. They're content with a typical version of happily ever after."

And now my question had set Johanna's sights on Jillian. Should I ignore the unspoken criticism or not? "You don't approve of Geoff?"

"I wouldn't marry him. They remind me of that old nursery rhyme. 'Jack Sprat could eat no fat, his wife could eat no lean . . .'"

"And I suppose one of the reasons you're marrying Beckett is because you make such a good-looking couple?"

"You've got to admit he's easy on the eyes."

Easy on the eyes? Who said stuff like that anymore? "Not that he's around very often for anyone to get a look at him."

"If I don't mind being in a long-distance relationship, I don't see why you should be so critical." Johanna's stilettos tapped a sharp staccato on the wood floor, her platinum-blonde hair caught up in a tight ponytail that swished down between her shoulder blades.

"I'm not criticizing. Just mentioning that Beckett plays the role of the Invisible Man quite well."

"You're almost as funny as Geoff." Ice frosted Johanna's words.

Time to change the subject again unless I wanted a full-blown argument with one sister during my other sister's party. Not that I could think of a topic Johanna and I agreed on. "Isn't it odd? You and Beckett have been engaged for over two years now. Shouldn't we be planning your wedding so Jillian and Geoff don't beat you two down the aisle?"

"It's not a race. Beckett's stationed in Wyoming and I don't want to give up my job to move there—"

"Did I know Beckett was in Wyoming?"

"Honestly, Payton, he's been there for a year." Johanna sniffed. "But then, it's not like we chat every other day, is it? You and Pepper were the close ones—"

Heat flushed my neck. My face. "There's no need to bring Pepper into the conversation, is there?"

"Why, after all this time, are you still so sensitive about talking about her?"

"I'm not sensitive. I just don't see why you had to mention Pepper when we were talking about you and Beckett—"

The sound of voices rose once again as the kitchen door opened. Poor Kimberlee. She didn't know she'd have to assume Jillian's usual position as the neutral zone between Johanna and me.

"Have you seen Jillian?"

Not Kimberlee. Mom, who was also an expert human buffer.

"Isn't she with Geoff?" I removed the cling wrap from the cheesecake.

"She was a few moments ago, but now I can't find her." Mom circled the island as if she expected to find her middle daughter crouching down hiding from her. "Isn't it almost time for dessert? And aren't we supposed to open gifts after that? They certainly received a lot of presents, didn't they?"

"Yes. It's a great turnout." If only the kitchen didn't feel like a revolving three-ring circus. How would Johanna like it if our family showed up at the hospital pharmacy where she was in charge?

Before I could say anything else, Kimberlee, the one person I'd been waiting for, joined the crowd. "Are we all set in here, Payton?"

"Just about." I swallowed back the words *"if people would stay out of my kitchen."* This wasn't my kitchen. And family or not, Mom was a client, at least for tonight, and needed to be treated like one. And I'd been dealing with Johanna for years. If I wanted tonight to be a success, the less said, the better.

"Mom, why don't you and Johanna join the guests?" I removed the classic cheesecake from the fridge. "I'll find Jillian while Kimberlee makes the announcement about dessert and Jillian and Geoff opening their gifts."

As Johanna and Mom left, I faced my business partner, shook my head, and sighed. "Family. And before that, a longtime family friend wandered in, asking for the crab dip recipe."

"It comes with working for relatives." Kimberlee took the cheesecake from me, the eclectic assortment of rings on her fingers sparkling under the kitchen lights. "But honestly, everything has gone beautifully. There's hardly any food left."

"That's because I know how to plan portions."

"It's because we know how to throw a good party."

"Well, let's keep things going and get this dessert set up."

Once the trio of cheesecakes was arranged on the table in my parents' dining room, I nodded to Kimberlee. "I've got to go find our bride-to-be."

"No problem. I can handle this." Kimberlee smoothed a wrinkle from the white tablecloth and repositioned the vase filled with bright-red poppies, my mother's favorite flowers.

"It's not like she wandered far. She's probably in the bathroom touching up her makeup."

Not that Jillian was a "refresh her makeup" kind of gal. Mascara and a little bit of basic eyeliner was her usual routine. Lipstick was reserved for fancier affairs. She'd probably be cajoled by the photographer into wearing some on her wedding day.

The upstairs bathroom was empty, lit only by the flickering flame of a cinnamon-scented candle. Where could Jillian be? A thin band of light shone out from beneath the door of Johanna and Jillian's former bedroom at the far end of the darkened hallway. Why would my sister be in there? As I moved past my old bedroom, my fingertips brushed the doorknob for a second. I pulled my hand away, balling my fingers into a fist.

I paused outside the bedroom and then rapped my knuckles against the door. "Jillian?"

Nothing . . . and then, "Payton? Do you need me for something?"

Just for her party. I eased the door open, stepping inside. "What are you doing up here? It's time to open your gifts."

What had once been Johanna and Jillian's room was now a generic guest room. At the moment, the only light came from the slender glass lamp on the bedside table. My sisters' beds had been replaced by a single larger bed covered in a gray-and-white paisley comforter. An idyllic outdoor scene adorned the wall across from the dark oak dresser.

Jillian, who'd been hunched over on the corner of the bed, straightened her shoulders. "I, um, got a phone call and decided to take it in here away from all the noise."

"Is everything okay?"

"Yes. Absolutely." Jillian's smile seemed to wobble for the briefest second. "Did you need me for something?"

"Your engagement party? It's time to dismantle that Jenga tower of gifts in the family room." I shook my head. "*Tsk*. And after all the hard work I put in arranging it."

"Right." Jillian smoothed her yellow empire-waist sundress down over her hips. "It's been a wonderful party, Payton."

"Thank you for saying so, but it's not over yet." I touched Jillian's shoulder. "You're really okay?"

She nodded so that the ends of her hair brushed against the back of my hand. "Yes. Nothing that won't wait until Monday."

I didn't know why I'd asked. It wasn't like Jillian would confide in me. We weren't the "Will you keep a secret?" kind of sisters. "All right then. Why don't you go find Geoff and I'll bring you both some dessert? Do you want key lime, classic, or turtle cheesecake?"

Now it was my sister's turn to shake her head. "I should skip it altogether. We're going wedding dress shopping soon enough, and I know I'm going to look awful—"

"Oh, stop! Don't become a weight-conscious bridezilla." My comment earned the ghost of a laugh from my sister. "What's wrong?"

"You know Mrs. Kenton?"

"Of course—the family friend who can get away with saying, 'Oh, Payton, I knew you when . . .' and does. Every time she sees me. She pull that on you tonight?"

Red stained my sister's face. "No. She just said—in

the nicest way possible, of course—that she hoped I'd lose a few pounds before the wedding."

"And what did you say?"

"Nothing."

Of course she didn't. "Jillian—"

She waved away my words. "Forget I said anything."

"It was rude." And Mrs. Kenton, family friend or not, could forget about ever seeing the recipe she'd requested. "How about I bring you a small slice of each cheesecake? Calories don't count at engagement parties, you know."

"Really small slices?"

"I promise. This is a celebration. Your one and only engagement party."

"You're right." Jillian stood, brushing her straight hair away from her face. "Tonight, we celebrate. Tomorrow . . . well, we're not thinking about that, are we?"

"No, because tomorrow means playing catch-up for me. And prepping for next week."

And Saturday morning breakfast with my family.

Something else I wasn't thinking about.

Breakfast at my parents' always required drinking at least three cups of coffee.

I retrieved the glass coffeepot from the kitchen and brought it to the table, pouring a steady stream of dark liquid fortitude into the Dallas Starbucks mug from one of Dad's business trips. A trip equaled a coffee mug. Just like everything in the kitchen, the coffeemaker was outdated. Maybe I could convince my sisters to buy our parents a Keurig for Christmas. "Anyone else need a refill?"

Only Dad nodded, moving his faded orange-and-blue Broncos mug closer to me so I could add coffee, the roasted aroma filling the air. After returning the pot to its proper place, I slid into my chair across from Johanna and began sweetening my coffee.

"Three sugars? What is that, your second cup of coffee?" Johanna wrinkled her nose. "Have you ever heard of Splenda or Stevia?"

"My third. And I prefer the real stuff. I like my caffeine with a jolt of sugar." I stirred the overabundance of sugar, my spoon clinking against the rim.

"I'm surprised your teeth haven't rotted out of your head."

My fingers tightened around the handle of my mug. "Well, if they did, I'd be the one paying my dental bills—"

"Really, girls, it's barely ten o'clock in the morning," Mom interrupted the exchange. "And you're both adults. Stop bickering."

"Weren't we discussing the bridal shower?" Dad's tone was even.

"We've discussed the basics." Johanna scanned the list she'd made on her iPad. "With the wedding in April, we could wait until February for the shower. Or we could do something sooner, say November, and let your friends and coworkers host another shower closer to the wedding date. As maid of honor, I'll be hosting this party, of course, with Payton and Kimberlee's company catering it."

"As long as Jillian's happy with all that." I resisted the urge to toss a fourth spoonful of sugar into my coffee. I could either hassle my oldest sister or drink my much-needed eye-opener in peace.

"I'm sorry—what?" Jillian yawned and moved left-over scrambled eggs around her plate with her fork.

"I just said Kimberlee and I are happy to cater the bridal shower so long as you're good with that."

"Oh . . . of course. I loved all the appetizers you served."

"The bison sliders were awesome." Geoff spoke around a bite of bacon.

"I wouldn't want anyone else to do my bridal shower." Jillian smiled when Geoff reached over and squeezed her hand. "But, Payton, could you work something out so you can attend the party, too? I hardly saw you last night."

"I was there when you opened gifts—well, most of them." I pressed my fingertips into the knots at the base of my neck. The consequence of setup, cleanup, and loading supplies into the business van Kimberlee drove back to North Denver last night. "I'll see if we can arrange things so I can be around for more of the actual bridal shower. We can always bring in other people to help."

Johanna added something to her list. "I'll get together more specifics about a theme, food, and decor and e-mail you, Payton. And then Jillian just needs to let us know a preferred date."

"That'll be fine." I glanced up from a text from Nash asking when I'd be getting home. Let Johanna take the lead and relegate me to the background. That was easiest. "If we're done here, I'll finish my coffee and hit the road . . ."

Mom shifted in her chair. "There is one more thing we need to talk about."

"There is?"

"Yes. I, um, got a phone call—" Mom made eye contact with everyone at the table but me—"from Pepper's high school volleyball coach. Your coach."

My phone slipped from my hand, bouncing off the edge of the table and tumbling to the faux Persian carpet with a soft thud. "Coach Sydney? Why would she call you?"

Now Mom looked at me, then concentrated on setting her silverware on her empty plate, one piece at a time. "Well, she wanted to tell me the high school is honoring some of their former outstanding athletes. And Pepper is included because of all the school records she set. They plan on retiring her jersey number and displaying it in the gym."

My hands gripped my jeans-covered knees, and I willed myself to remain still as Mom talked. It was no surprise the school would honor a star athlete like Pepper. Several college coaches had been keeping track of her statistics by the time she was a sophomore.

Mom twisted a strand of her brown hair that was threaded through with gray. "Remember how they called you and Pepper—?"

"Double Trouble." I whispered the nickname given us by some of our opponents because Pepper and I were identical twins, and we both played middle.

"That's right. It was always fun to read that in the paper." Even all these years later, Mom seemed to relish the memory. "Anyway, Sydney was trying to get in touch with you because she hopes you'll say something about Pepper at the ceremony."

Mom's request might as well have been a well-aimed dump by a setter—and me, one of the unsuspecting defenders on the other side of the volleyball net. "What? No. Surely they can do this ceremony without me being a part of it."

"Pepper was your twin sister, Payton. She was closer to you than anyone else."

"Mom, please!" I shoved my chair back, stumbling to my feet, almost stepping on my phone.

"Honey, it's been ten years since Pepper died—"

"I know how long it's been, Mom. That doesn't mean I want to talk about Pepper in front of a bunch of people I don't know or haven't seen in years."

"What is wrong with you?" And now Johanna had to join the conversation. "This is a chance to honor Pepper's memory. Why don't you want to be a part of it? Everyone else is on board."

"Am I the last one to know about this?" I forced myself to face my family instead of walking out of the room. Out of the house.

"Well, you don't visit that often, do you?" Johanna managed to twist the conversation away from honoring Pepper to skewering me. "Or call. This is the first chance we've had to talk with you about the ceremony."

I'd deal with today's unexpected issue and ignore Johanna's typical attack. "And you're all okay with this idea?"

"Payton, we're talking about one evening. A couple of hours at most." Dad's words were low. Steady. Ever the voice of reason. "We'll all be there together. Have a chance to remember Pepper and something that was important to her. And you, too. So yes, we all think this is a good idea."

"I don't have a choice?" Did anyone else think I sounded like a sulky adolescent?

"Of course you have a choice." Mom's smile held the hint of an apology. "We're not going to force you to participate—"

"But think of how it would look if we all attended and you didn't."

"Thank you so much for not forcing me, Johanna."

"Be an adult, Payton. Stop making this about you."

"But I'm the one expected to be up front, talking . . . about Pepper." I swallowed a sudden tightness in my throat.

I should have skipped breakfast and driven straight

home. Coming home was like trying to step into a faded family photograph—one that had been partially torn so that the image was incomplete. "When is this event taking place?"

"Sydney said it was scheduled for the middle of September." Mom twisted her napkin. "I have her phone number if you want to talk to her . . ."

Maybe surrender was my best option for dealing with this ambush—at least for now.

"Fine. I'll call her and get the details."

"You'll do it?"

I bent to retrieve my phone, trying to ignore the hope in Mom's voice. At least my overnight bag and purse were already by the front door. "I said I'd talk to her. I need to think about this more before I say yes. *If* I say yes. I need to make sure Kimberlee and I don't have a competing commitment." Maybe, just maybe, I'd get that lucky. "Text me her number, please. I need to head home. Nash is hoping to spend part of the day together —maybe catch a movie."

"Tell him we missed seeing him." Dad half rose from his chair.

"Of course." I came close enough for a quick hug, following that up with a similar duck and hug with Mom. "No need to walk me out. We'll talk soon."

As I backed up, I nodded to everyone else at the table, hoping a smile would suffice for a good-bye. "Have fun getting all that loot back to your apartment, Jillian."

"We will, but it's going to Geoff's house. He's got more room."

"Sounds like a plan."

Johanna didn't even look up from her iPad. "I'll be e-mailing you about the bridal shower, Payton."

"Fine." Another nod and then more distance.

Welcomed distance.

ABOUT THE AUTHOR

Beth K. Vogt believes God's best often waits behind the doors marked "Never." Having authored ten contemporary romance novels and novellas, *The Best We've Been*, the final book in Beth's Thatcher Sisters Series with Tyndale House Publishers, released May 2020. Other books in the women's fiction series include *Things I Never Told You*, which won the 2019 AWSA Award for Contemporary Novel of the Year, and *Moments We Forget*. Beth is a 2016 Christy Award winner, a 2016 ACFW Carol Award winner, and a 2015 RITA®finalist. An established magazine writer and former editor of the leadership magazine for MOPS International, Beth blogs for Learn How to Write a Novel and The Write Conversation and also enjoys speaking to writers group and mentoring other writers. Visit Beth and sign up for her free Words of Encouragement at bethvogt.com.

MORE BY BETH K. VOGT

For purchase options, visit www.bethvogt.com.

The Thatcher Sisters Series

Things I Never Told You

Moments We Forget

The Best We've Been

Destination Wedding Series

Crazy Little Thing Called Love

Almost Like Being in Love

You Can't Buy Me Love (e-novella)

You Can't Hurry Love (e-novella)

A Year of Weddings Novella

Autumn Brides: A November Bride

Stand Alone

Somebody Like You

Catch a Falling Star

Wish You Were Here

You Made Me Love You (e-novella)

Cover Design:

Hillary Manton Lodge Design